D1008595

Kochalka, James,
Johnny Boo and the
midnight monsters /
[2019].
33305247030020
sa   11/07/19

TOP SHELF PRODUCTIONS
MARIETTA, GA

Johnny Boo and the Midnight Monsters. © 2019 James Kochalka.

Published by Top Shelf Productions, PO Box 1282, Marietta, GA 30061-1282, USA. Top Shelf Productions is an imprint of IDW Publishing, a division of Idea and Design Works, LLC. Offices: 2765 Truxtun Road, San Diego, CA 92106. Top Shelf Productions®, the Top Shelf logo, Idea and Design Works®, and the IDW logo are registered trademarks of Idea and Design Works, LLC. All Rights Reserved. With the exception of small excerpts of artwork used for review purposes, none of the contents of this publication may be reprinted without the permission of IDW Publishing. IDW Publishing does not read or accept unsolicited submissions of ideas, stories, or artwork.

This is a work of fiction. Names, characters, businesses, places, events and incidents are either the products of the author's imagination or used in a fictitious manner. Any resemblance to actual persons, living or dead, or actual events is purely coincidental.

Editor-in-Chief: Chris Staros.

Edited by Leigh Walton.

Visit our online catalog at www.topshelfcomix.com.

Printed in Korea.

ISBN 978-1-60309-457-3

22   21   20   19   4   3   2   1

CHAPTER ONE

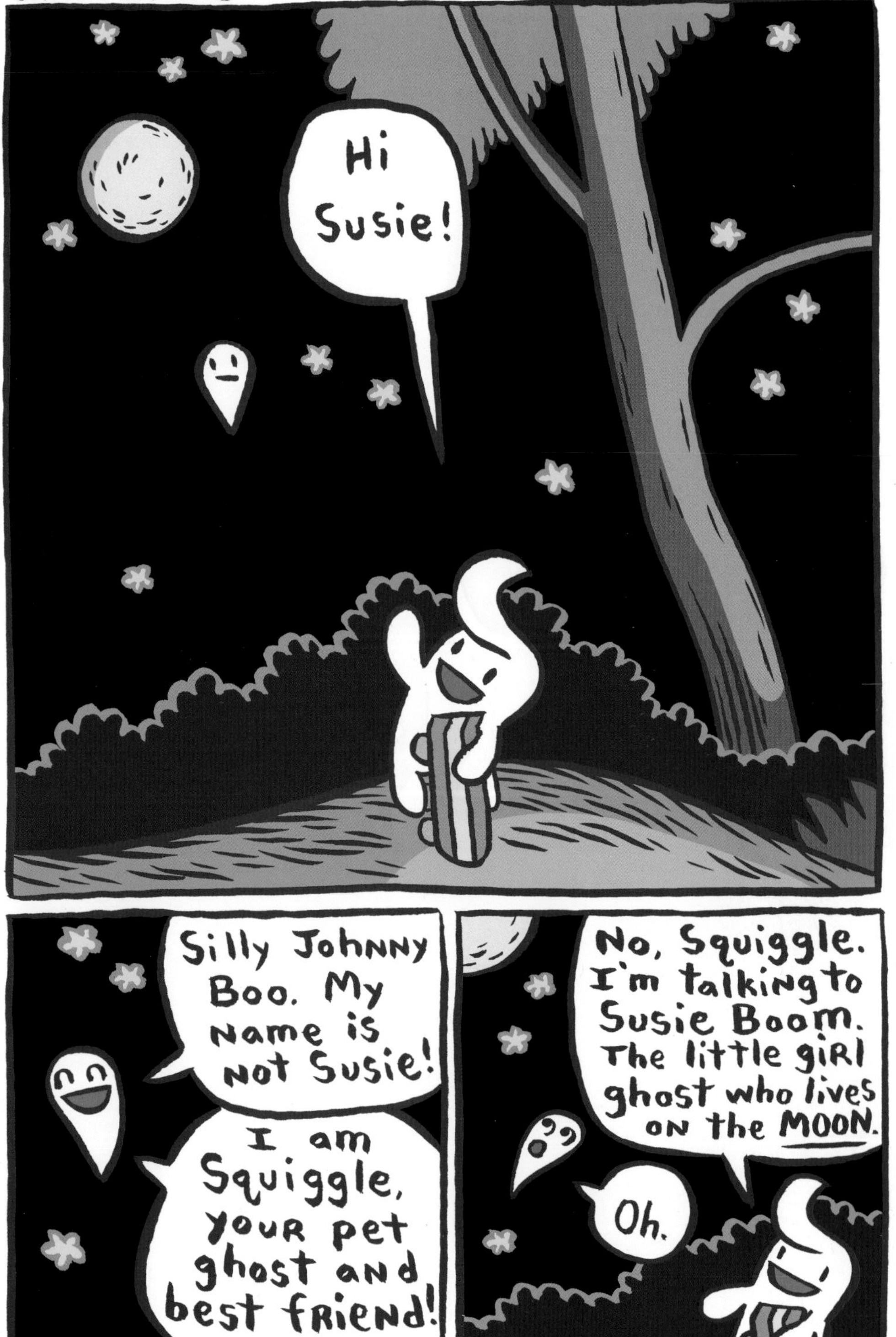
Hi Susie!
Silly Johnny Boo. My name is not Susie!
I am Squiggle, your pet ghost and best friend!
No, Squiggle. I'm talking to Susie Boom. The little girl ghost who lives on the MOON.
Oh.

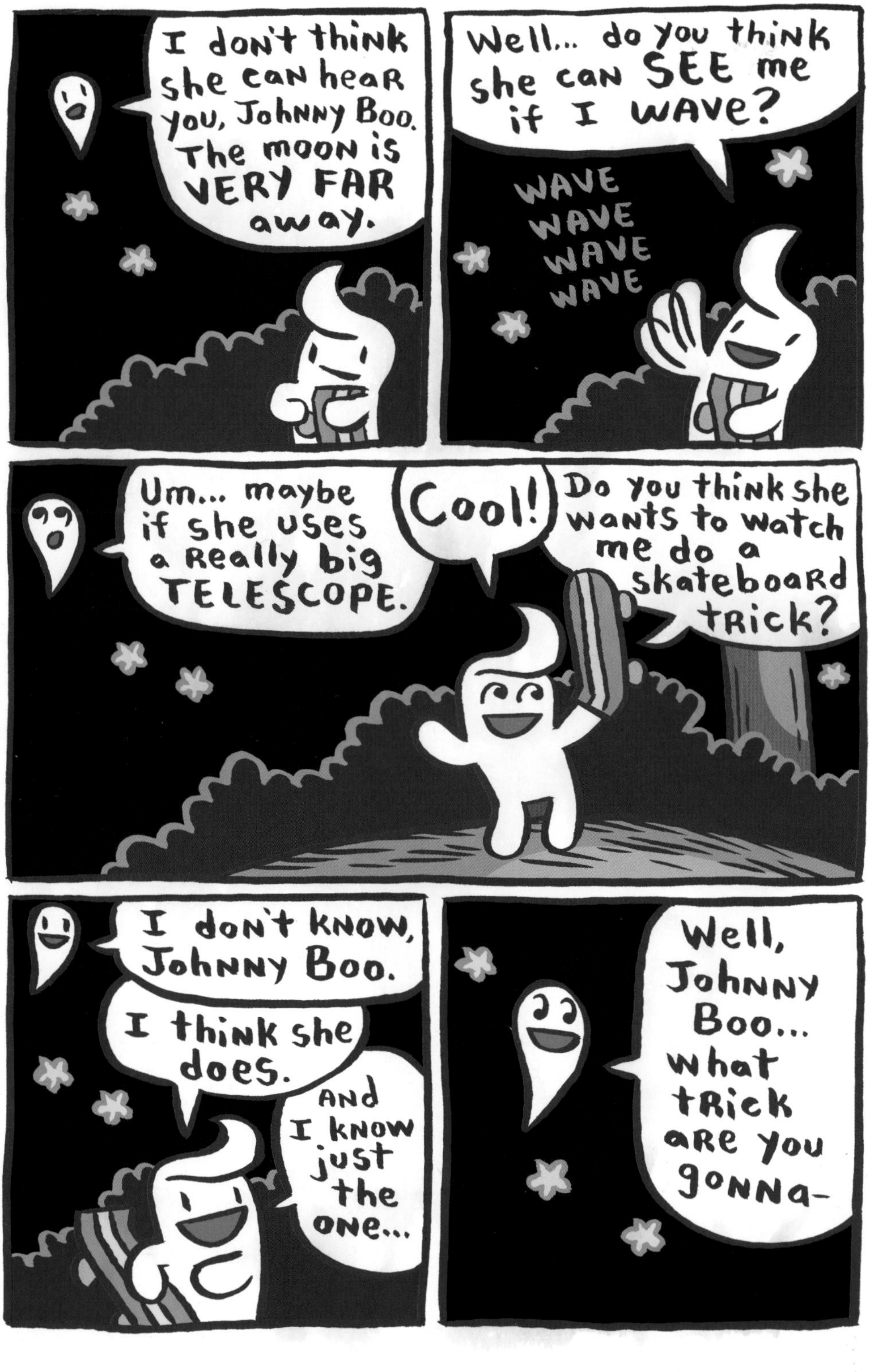
I don't think she can hear you, Johnny Boo. The moon is VERY FAR away.
Well... do you think she can SEE me if I WAVE?
WAVE WAVE WAVE WAVE
Um... maybe if she uses a really big TELESCOPE.
Cool!
Do you think she wants to watch me do a skateboard trick?
I don't know, Johnny Boo.
I think she does.
And I know just the one...
Well, Johnny Boo... what trick are you gonna-

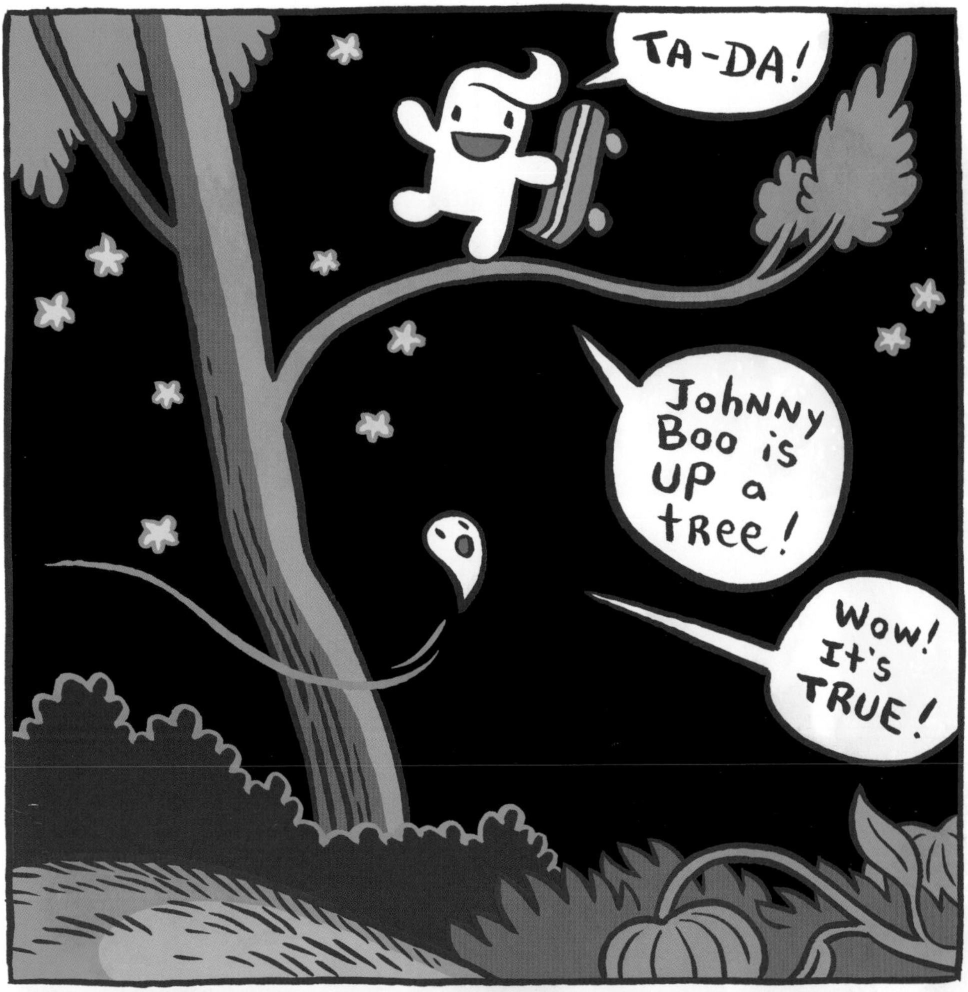
TA-DA!
Johnny Boo is UP a tree!
Wow! It's TRUE!

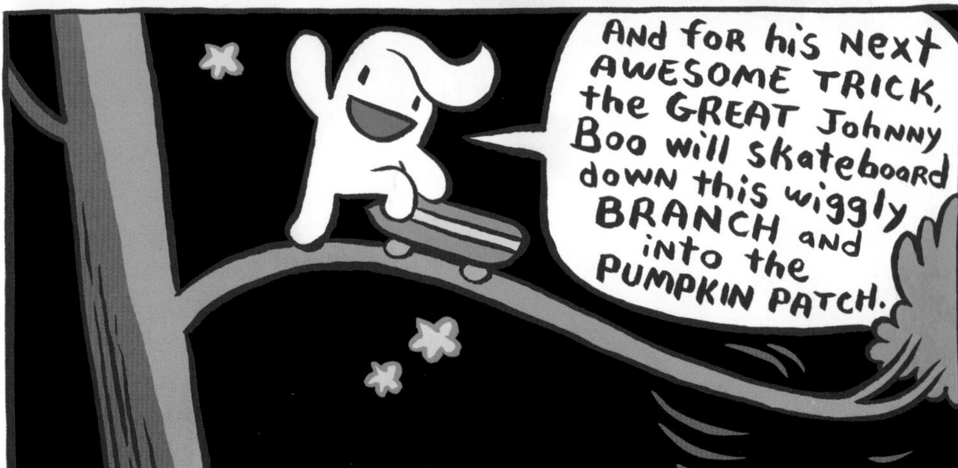
And for his Next AWESOME TRICK, the GREAT Johnny Boo will skateboard down this wiggly BRANCH and into the PUMPKIN PATCH.

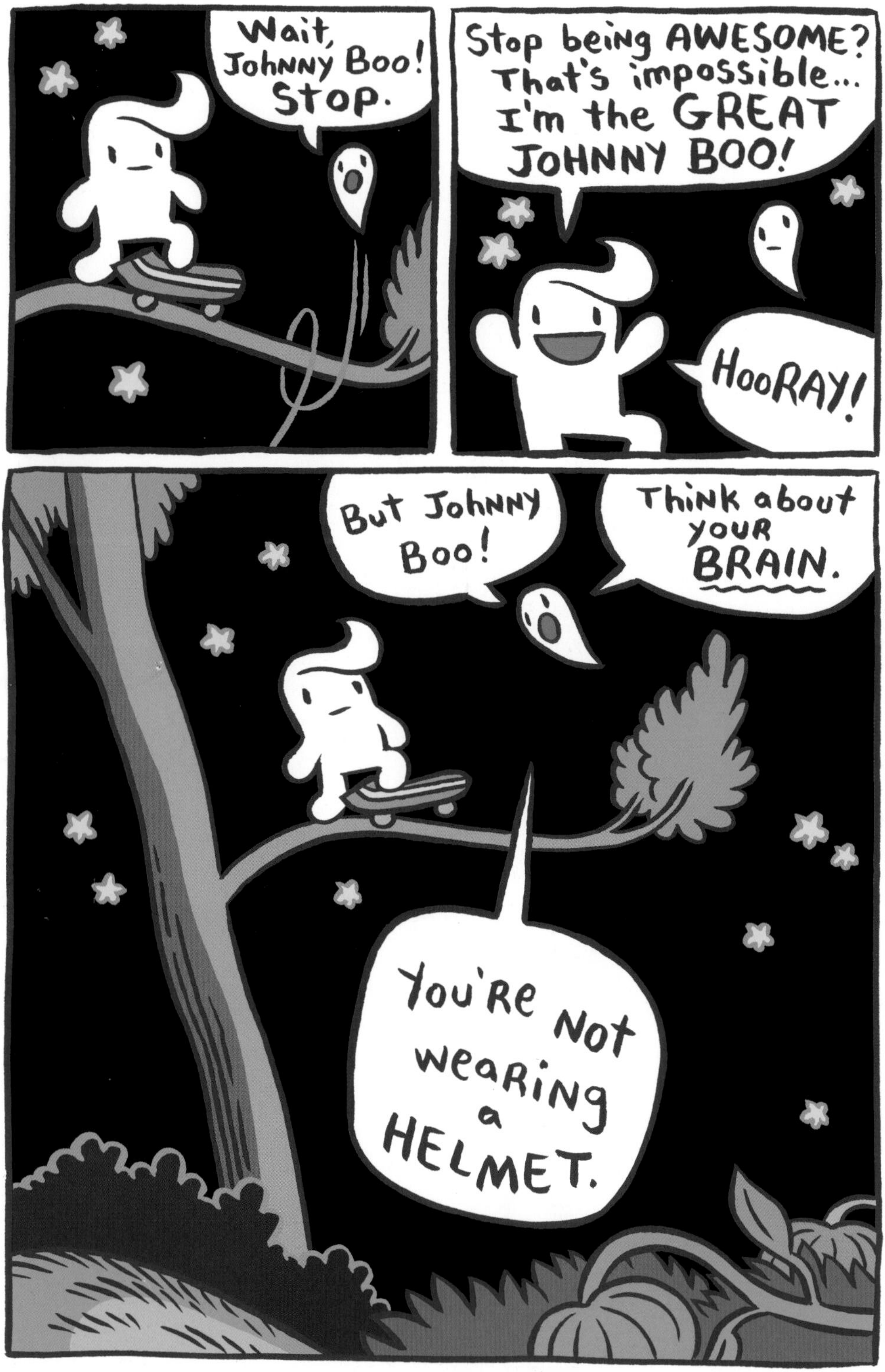
Wait, Johnny Boo! Stop.
Stop being AWESOME? That's impossible... I'm the GREAT JOHNNY BOO!
HooRAY!
But Johnny Boo!
Think about your BRAIN.
You're Not wearing a HELMET.

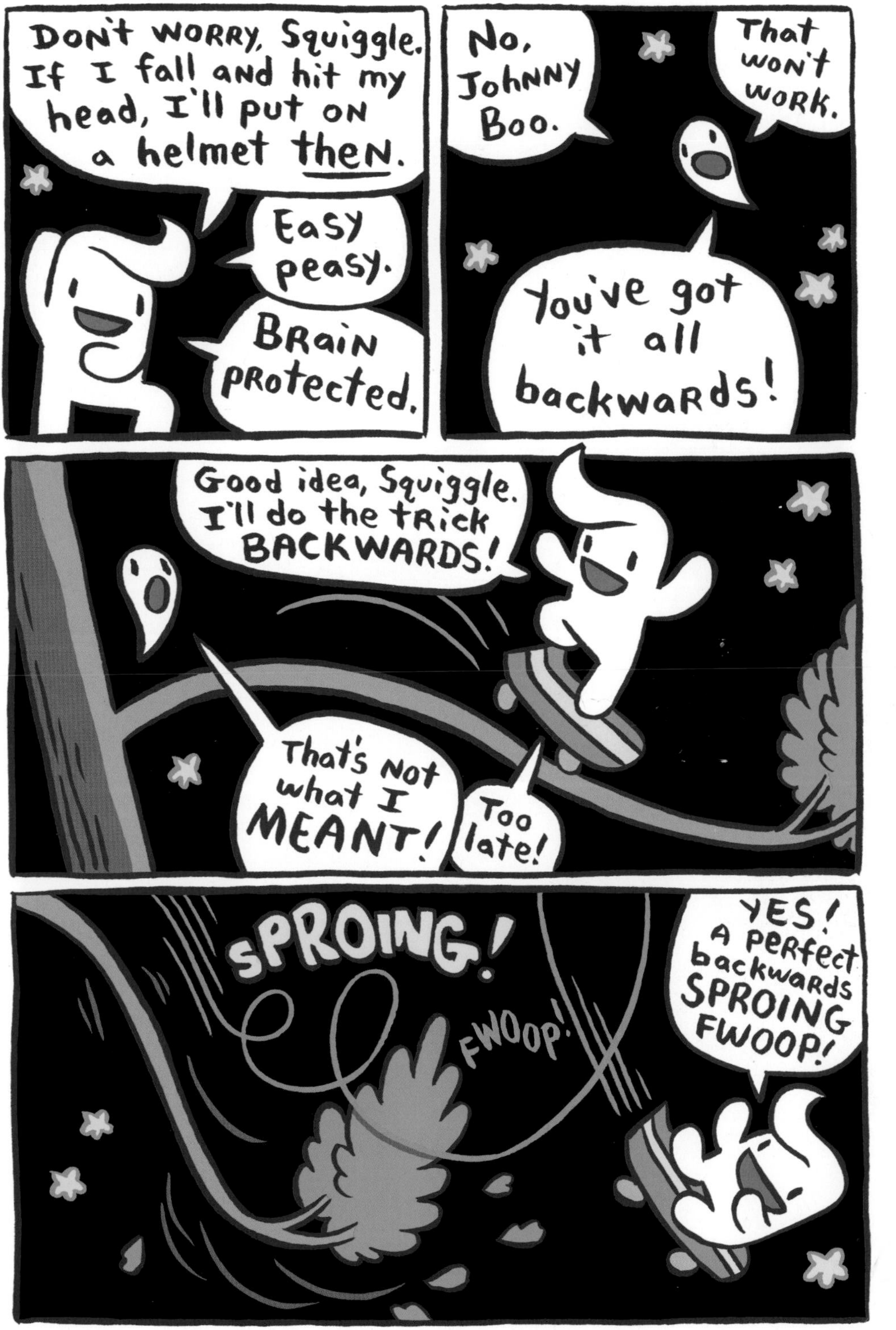
DON'T WORRY, Squiggle. If I fall and hit my head, I'll put ON a helmet thEN.
Easy peasy.
BRAIN protected.
No, JohNNY Boo.
That won't work.
You've got it all backwards!
Good idea, Squiggle. I'll do the tRick BACKWARDS!
That's NOT what I MEANT!
Too late!
sPROING!
FWOOP!
YES! A perfect backwards SPROING FWOOP!

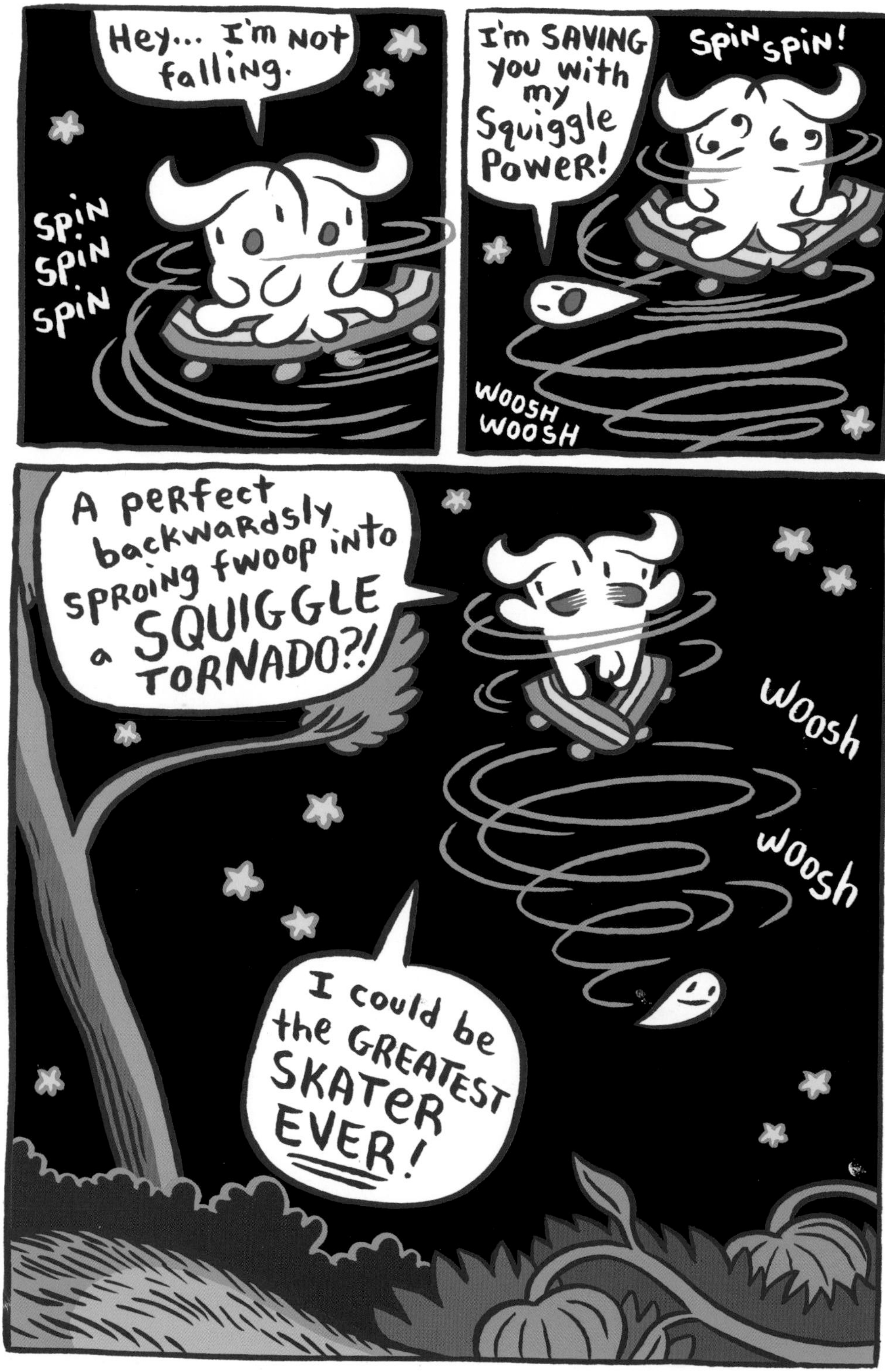
Hey... I'm not falling.
spin spin spin
I'm SAVING you with my Squiggle Power!
spin spin!
WOOSH WOOSH
A perfect backwardsly sproing fwoop into a SQUIGGLE TORNADO?!
woosh
woosh
I could be the GREATEST SKATER EVER!

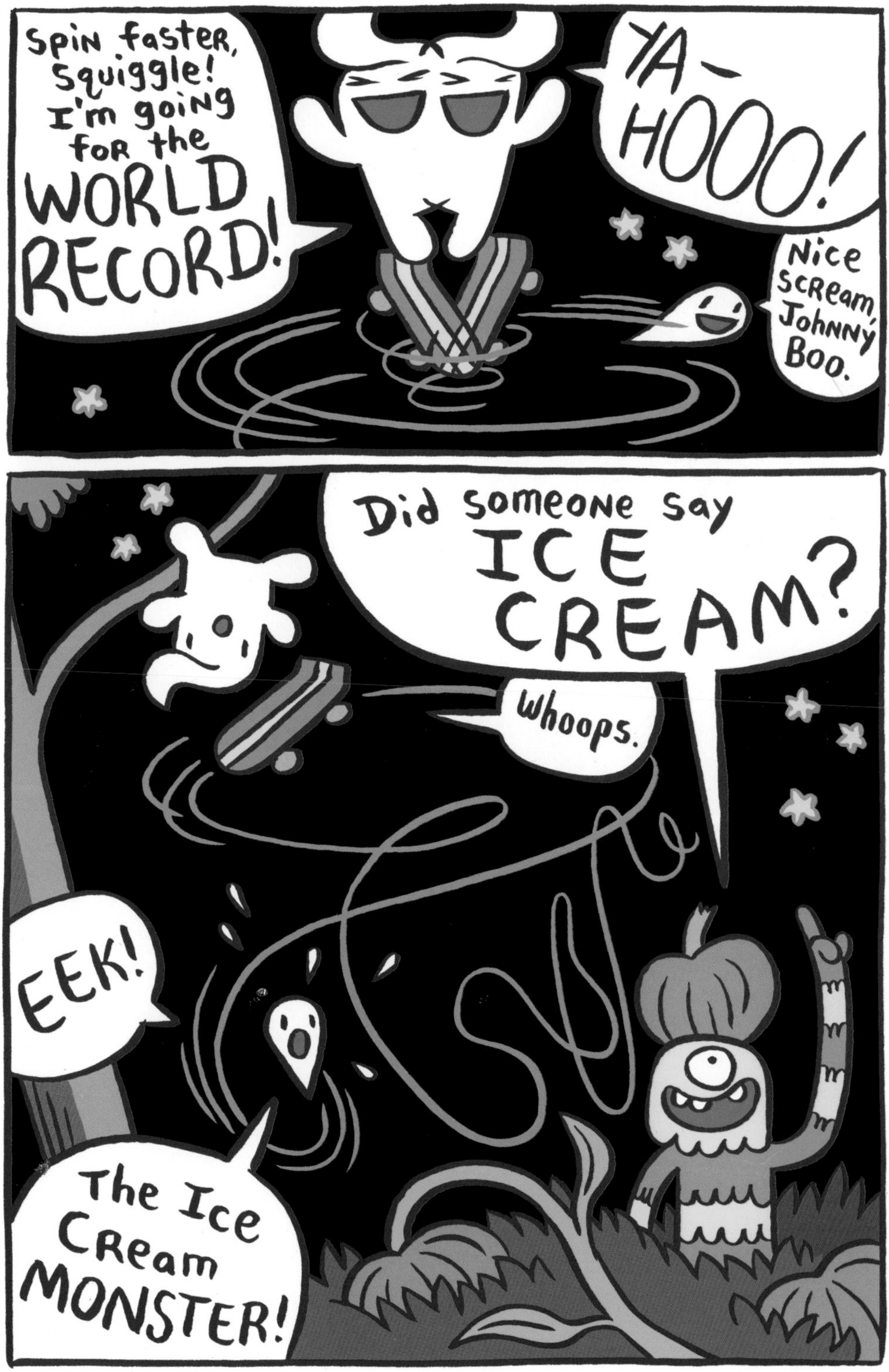

Spin faster, Squiggle! I'm going for the WORLD RECORD!
YA-HOOOO!
Nice scream, Johnny Boo.
Did someone say ICE CREAM?
Whoops.
EEK!
The Ice Cream MONSTER!

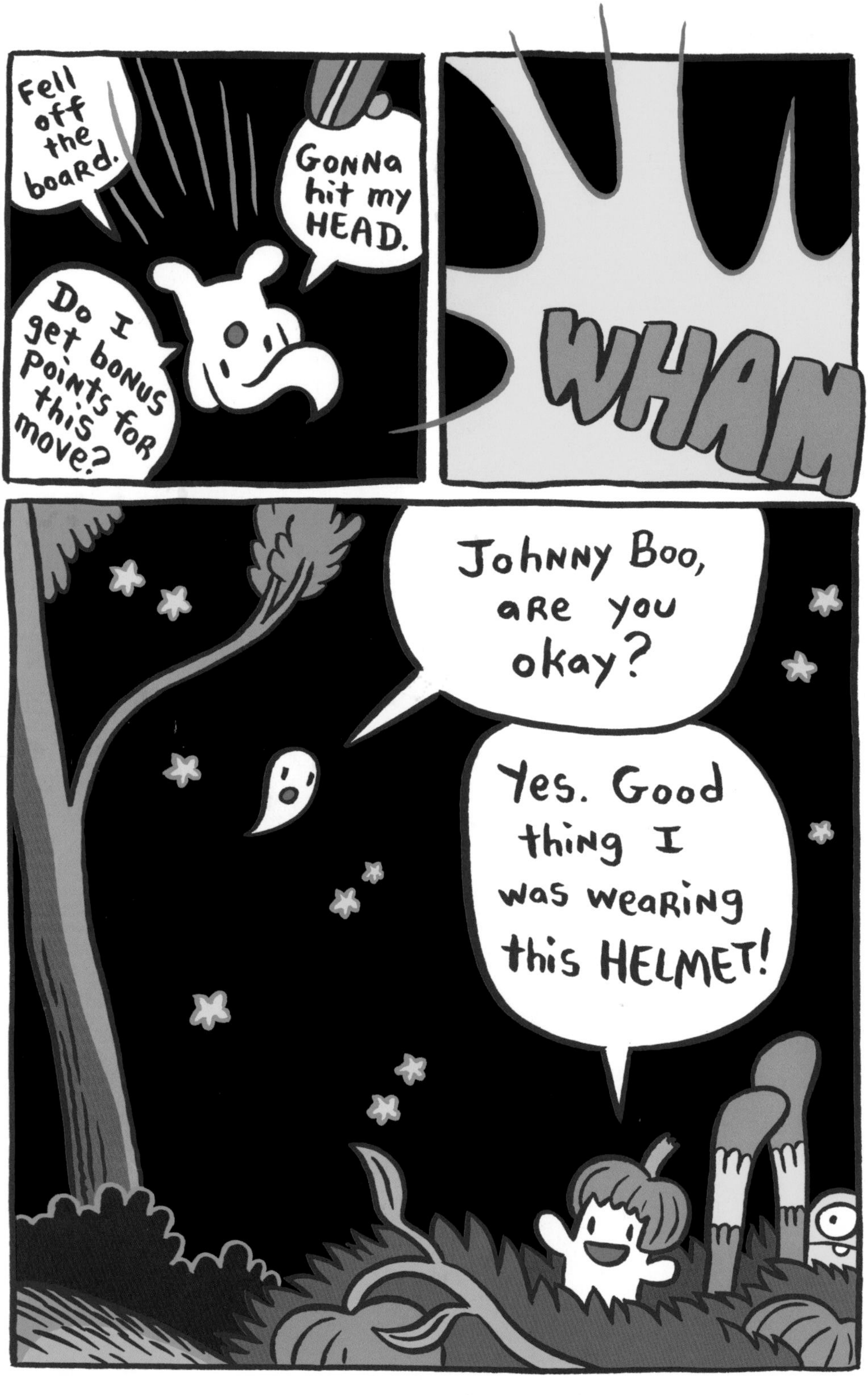
Fell off the board.
GONNa hit my HEAD.
Do I get bonus points for this move?
WHAM
Johnny Boo, are you okay?
Yes. Good thing I was wearing this HELMET!

CHAPTER TWO

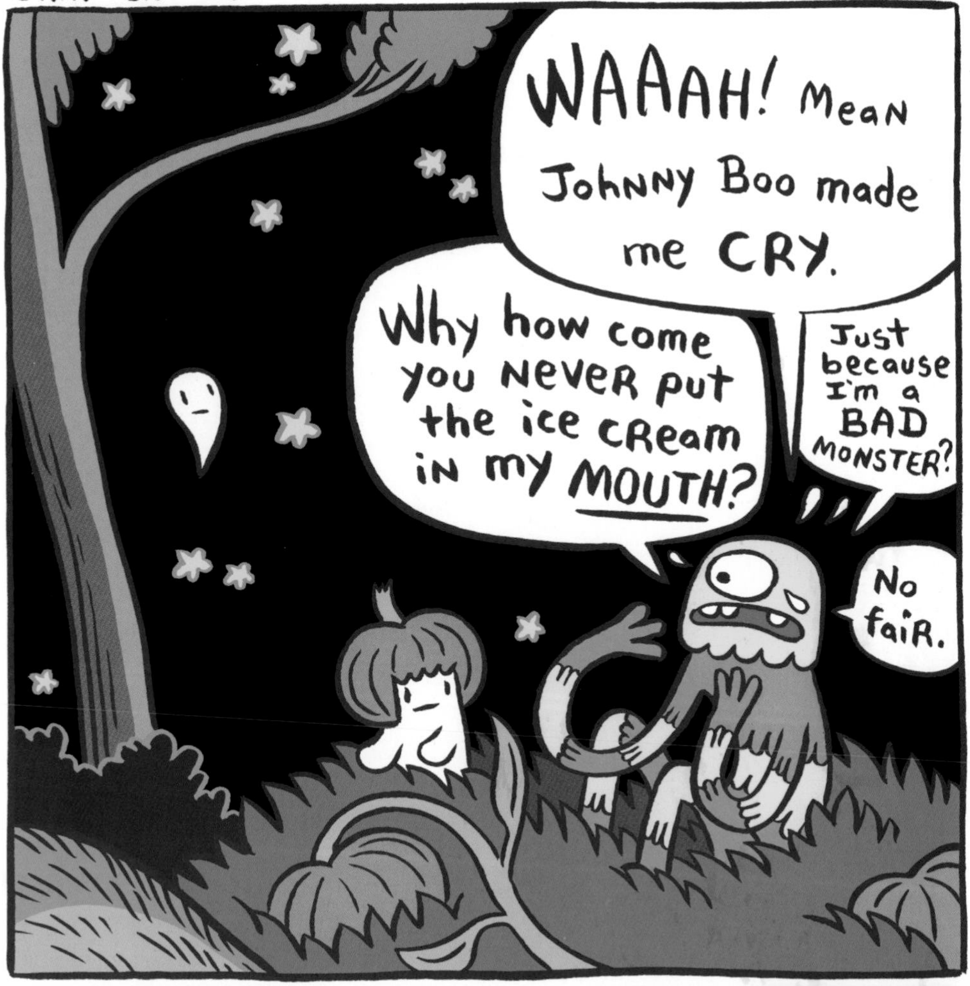
WAAAH! Mean Johnny Boo made me CRY.
Why how come you NEVER put the ice cream in my MOUTH?
Just because I'm a BAD MONSTER?
No fair.

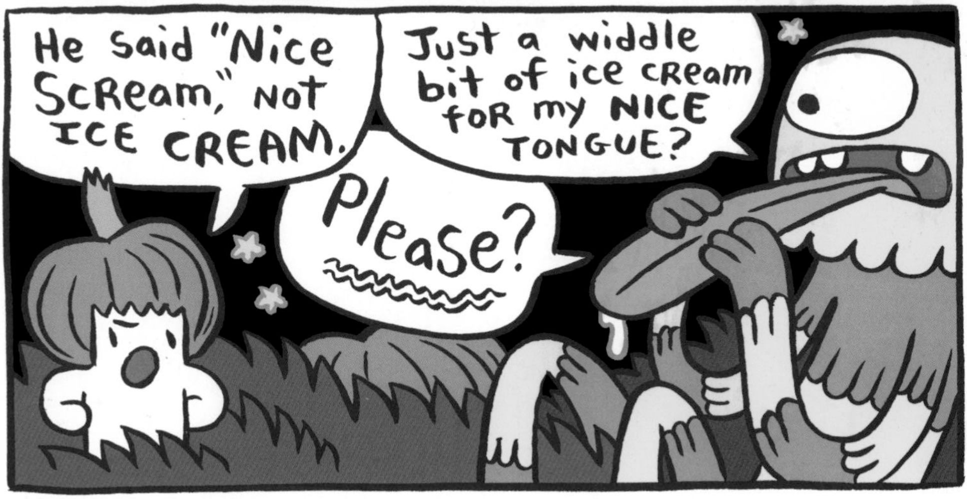
He said "Nice Scream," not ICE CREAM.
Just a widdle bit of ice cream for my NICE TONGUE?
Please?

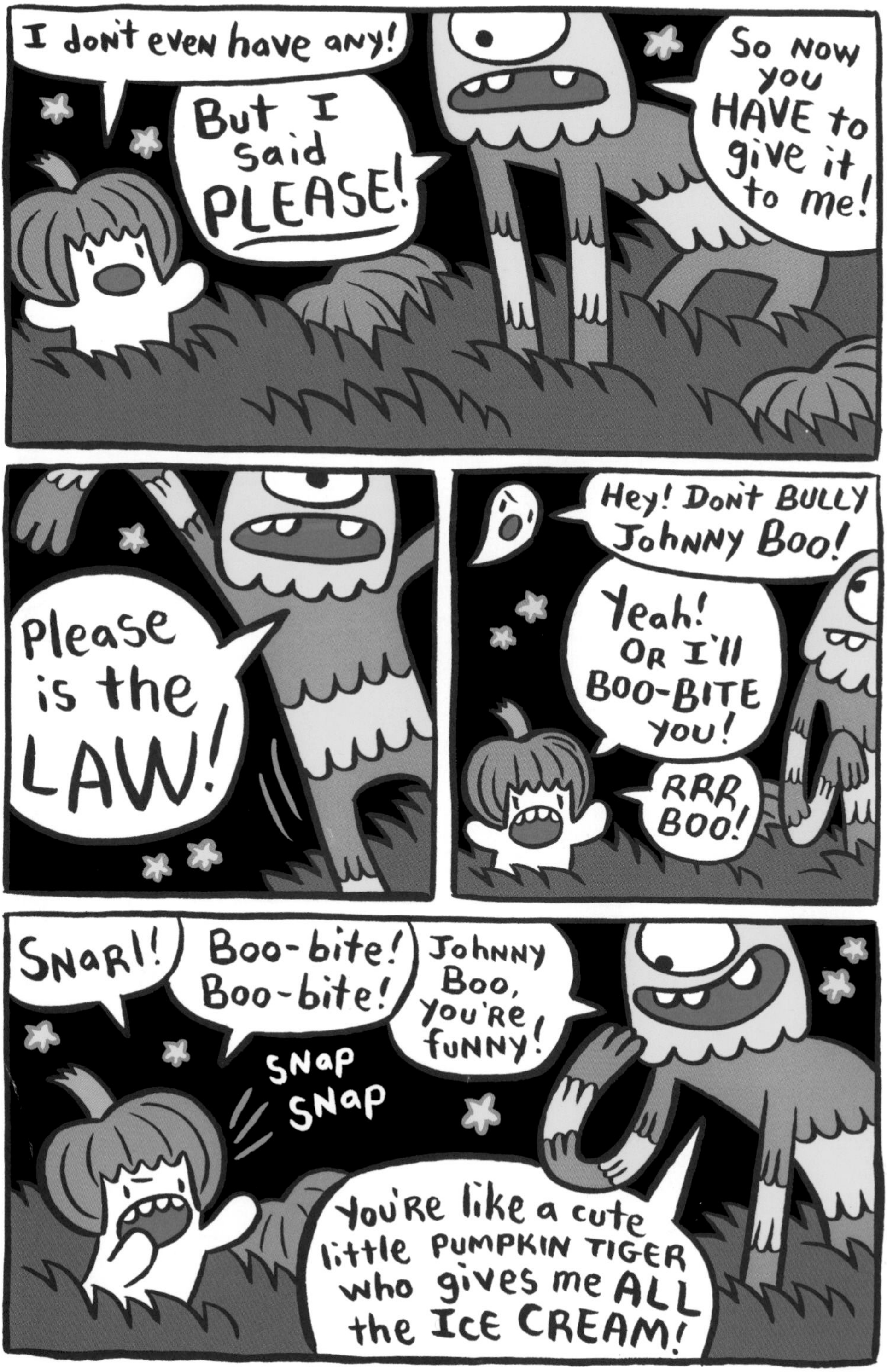
I don't even have any!
But I said PLEASE!
So now you HAVE to give it to me!
Please is the LAW!
Hey! Don't BULLY Johnny Boo!
Yeah! Or I'll BOO-BITE you!
RRR BOO!
Snarl!
Boo-bite! Boo-bite!
Johnny Boo, you're funny!
SNap SNap
You're like a cute little PUMPKIN TIGER who gives me ALL the ICE CREAM!

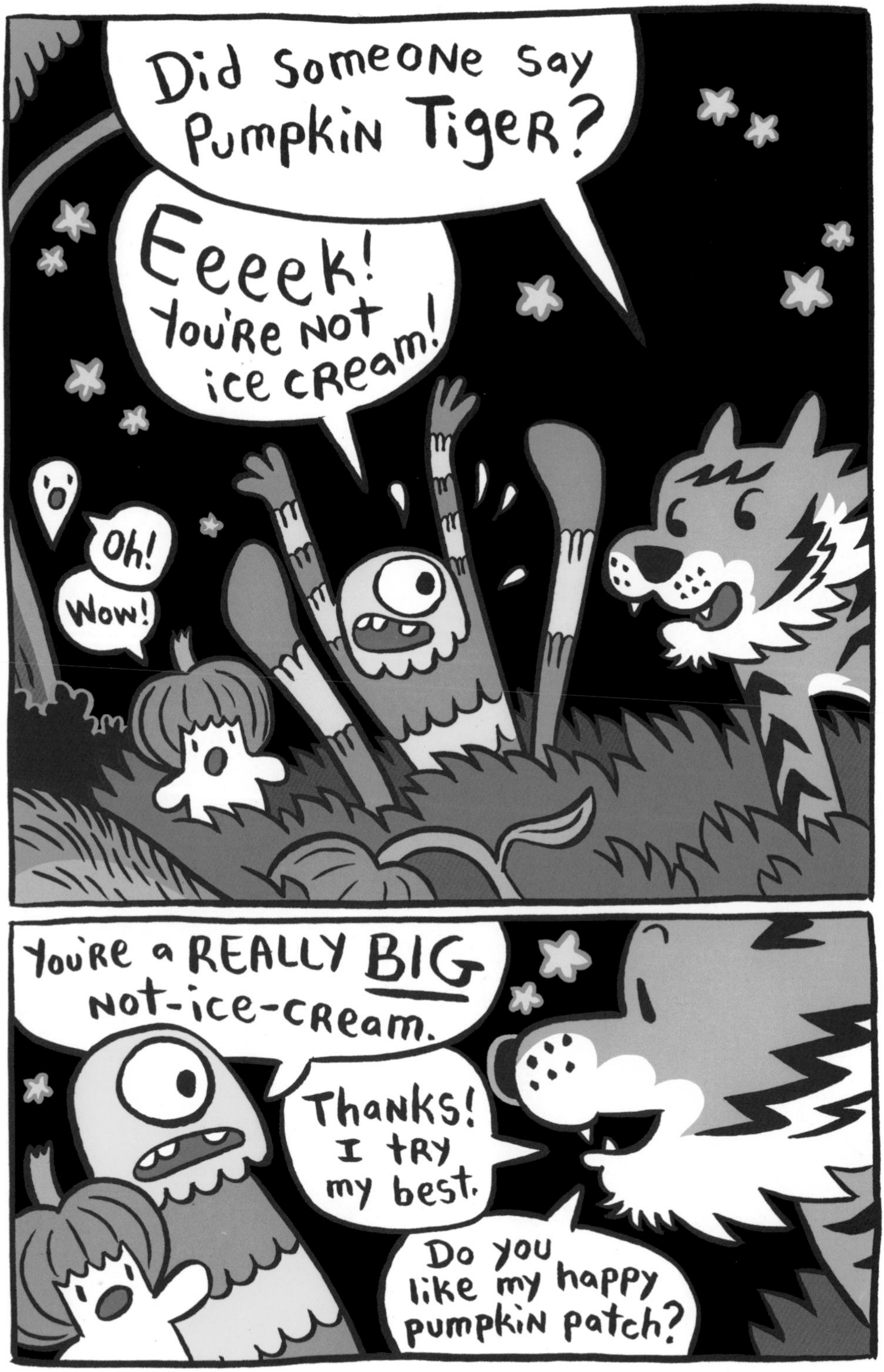
Did Someone say Pumpkin Tiger?
Eeeek! You're not ice cream!
Oh!
Wow!
You're a REALLY BIG not-ice-cream.
Thanks! I try my best.
Do you like my happy pumpkin patch?

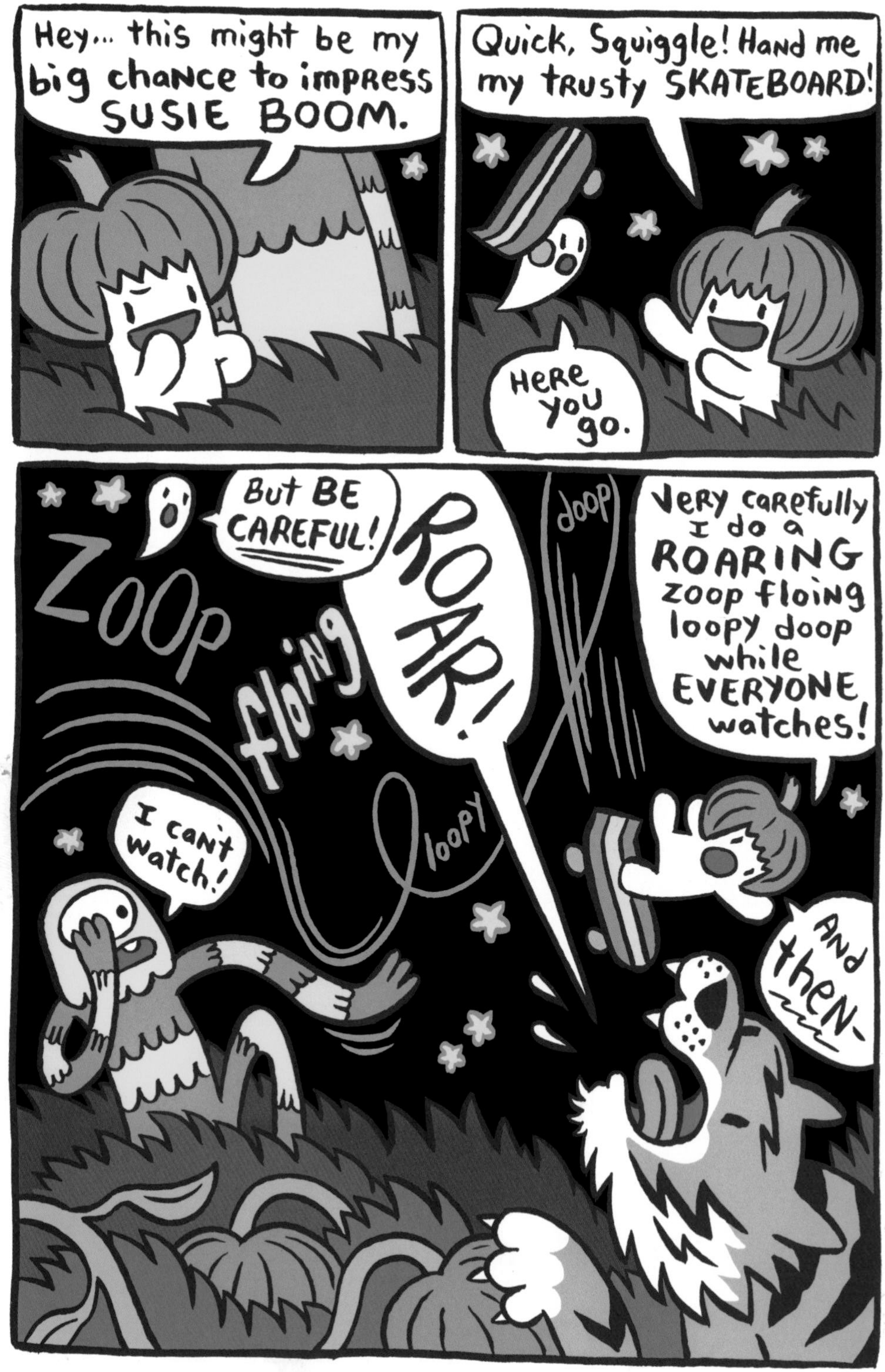
Hey... this might be my big chance to impress SUSIE BOOM.
Quick, Squiggle! Hand me my trusty SKATEBOARD!
Here you go.
But BE CAREFUL!
ZOOP
floing
ROAR!
loopy
doop
Very carefully I do a ROARING zoop floing loopy doop while EVERYONE watches!
I can't watch!
And then-

Wha ha ha ha hyurkle!
Johnny Boo skates a WILD TIGER!
AND then-
That tickles!

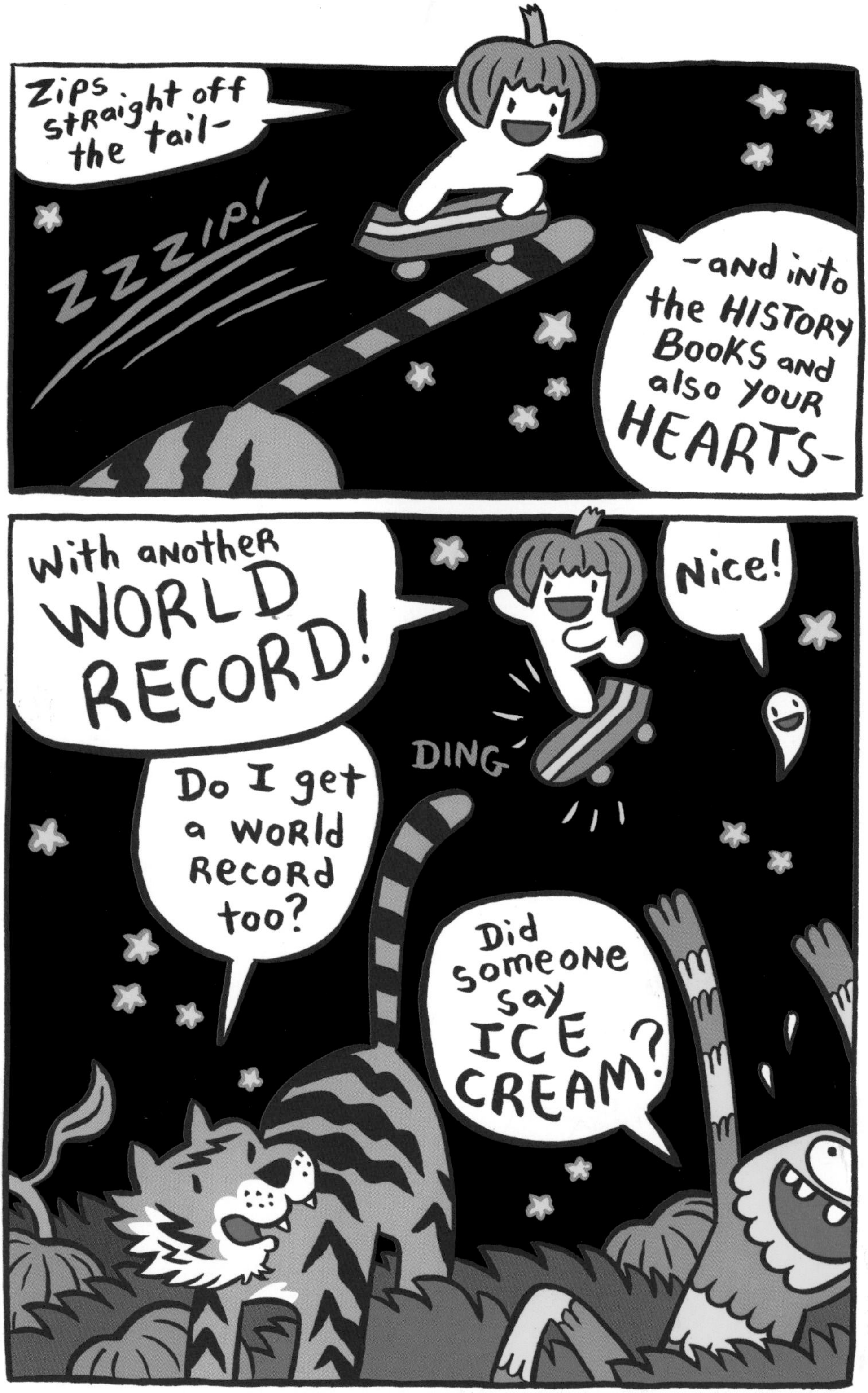
Zips straight off the tail-
ZZZIP!
-and into the HISTORY BOOKS and also YOUR HEARTS-
With another WORLD RECORD!
Nice!
DING
Do I get a WORLD Record too?
Did someone say ICE CREAM?

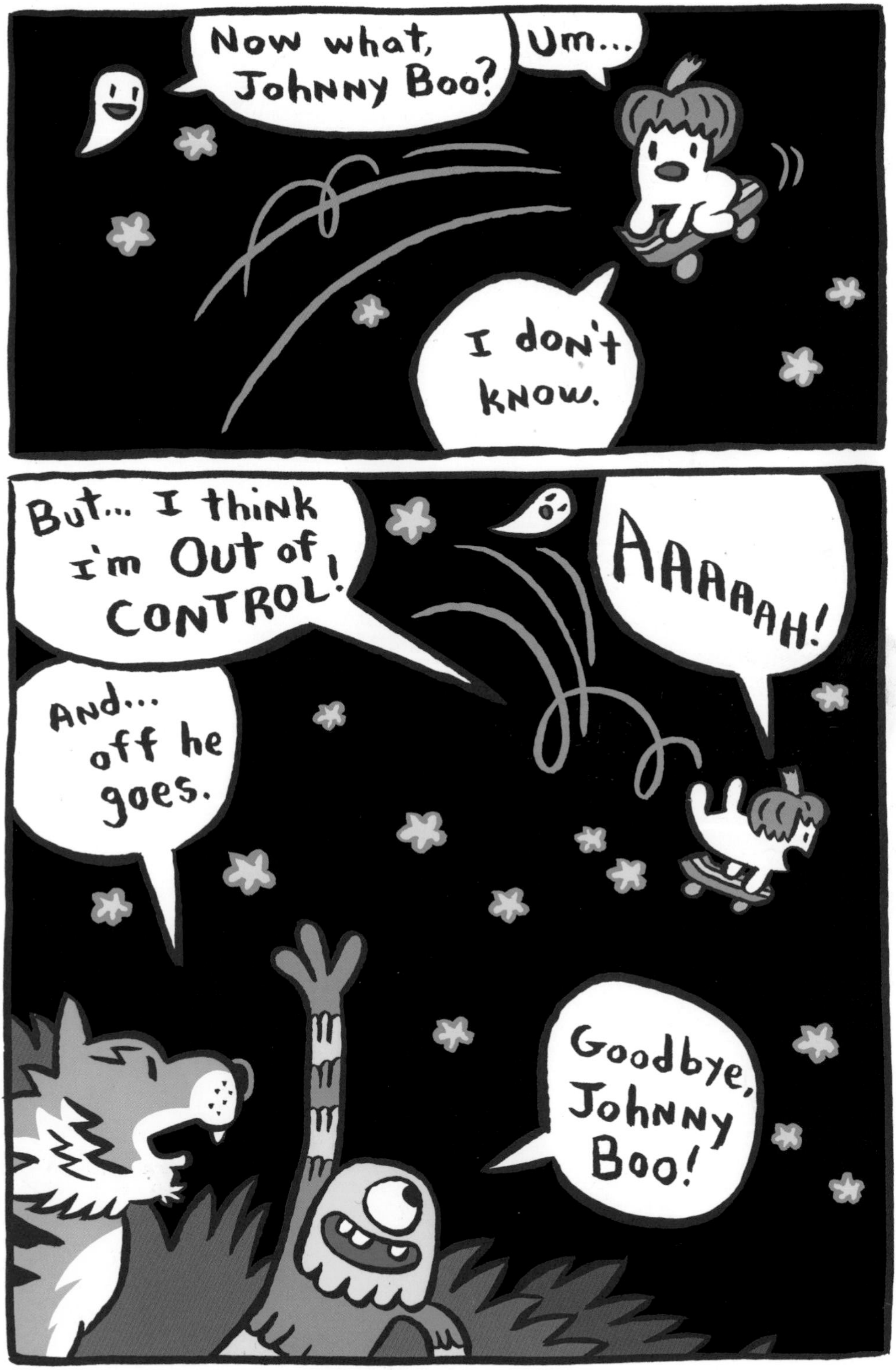
Now what, Johnny Boo?
Um...
I don't know.
But... I think i'm Out of CONTROL!
AAAAAAH!
And... off he goes.
Goodbye, Johnny Boo!

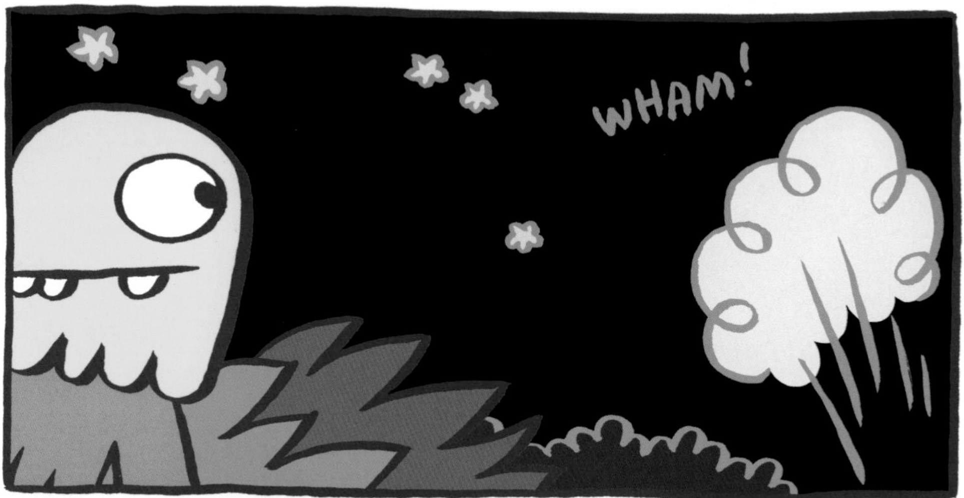
WHAM!

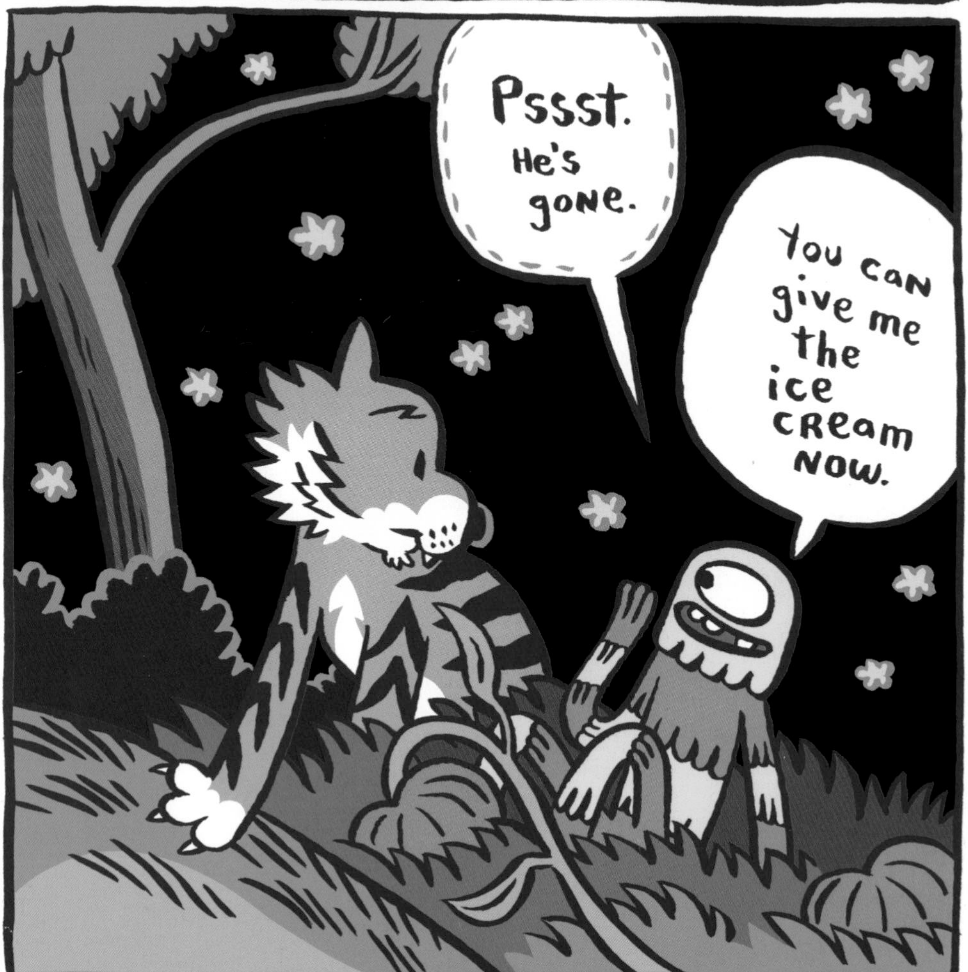
Pssst. He's gone.
You can give me the ice cream now.

CHAPTER THREE

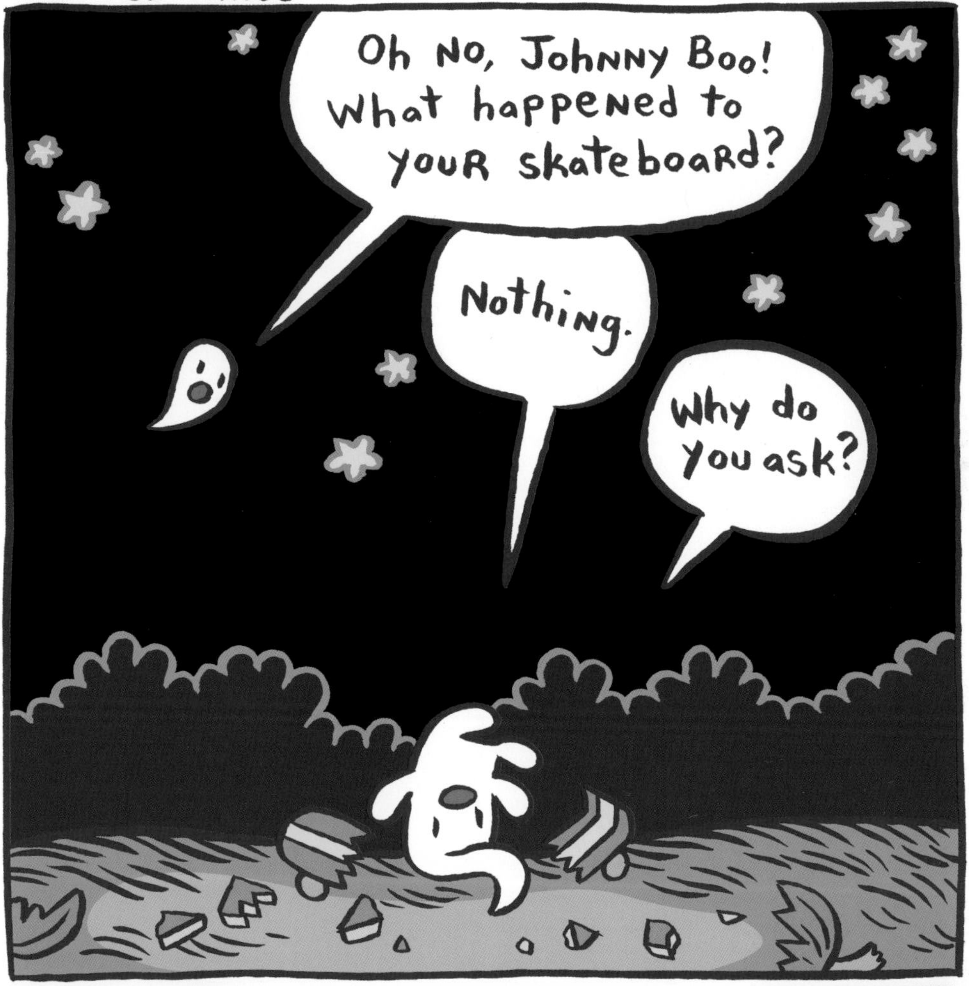
Oh No, Johnny Boo! What happened to your skateboard?
Nothing.
Why do you ask?

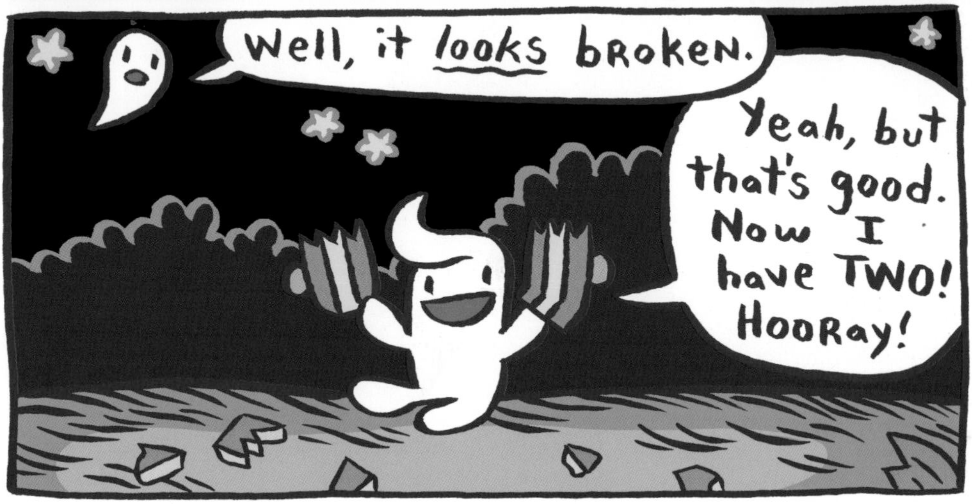
Well, it looks broken.
Yeah, but that's good. Now I have TWO! Hooray!

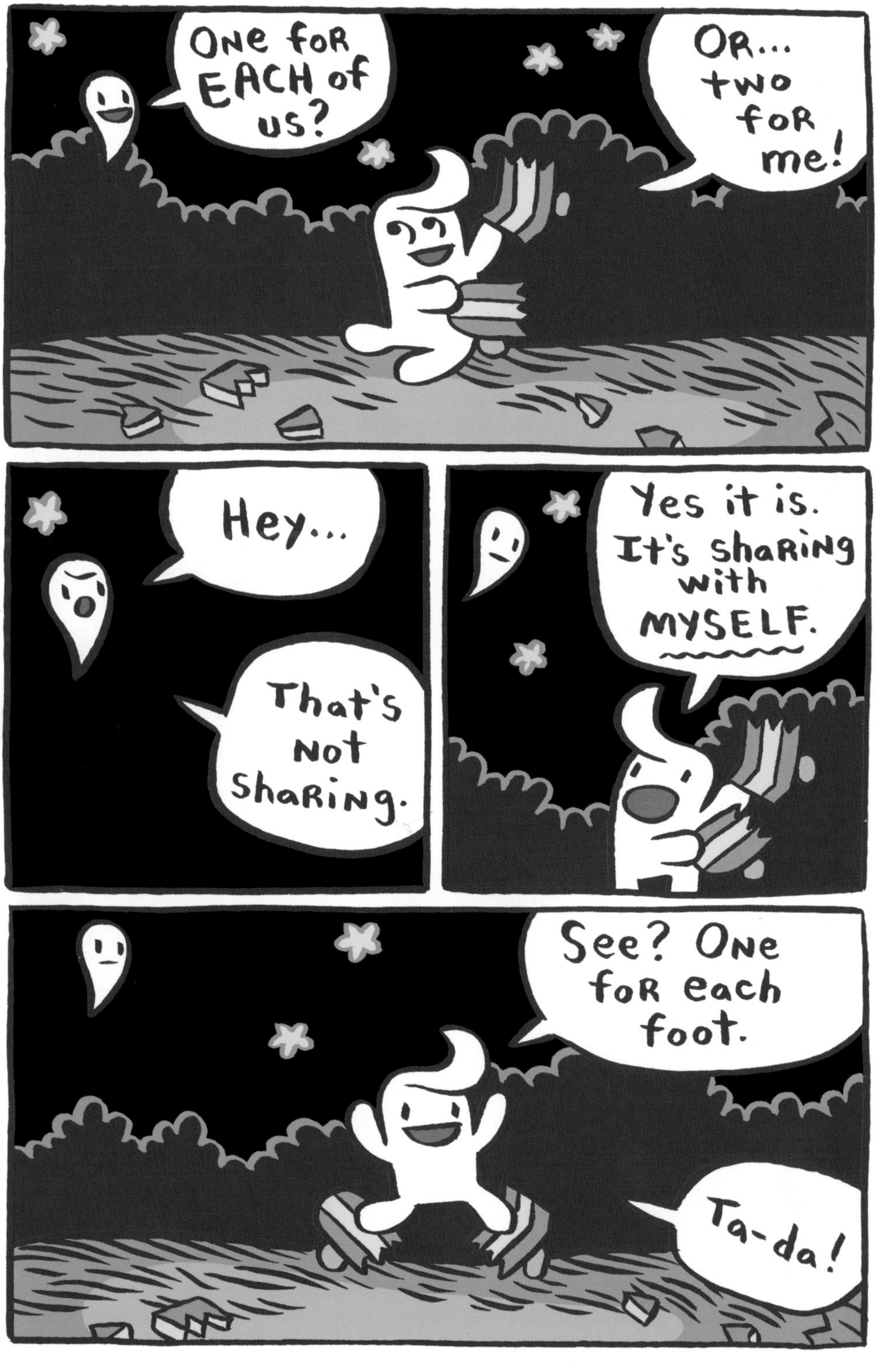
One for EACH of us?
OR... two for me!
Hey...
That's not sharing.
Yes it is. It's sharing with MYSELF.
See? One for each foot.
Ta-da!

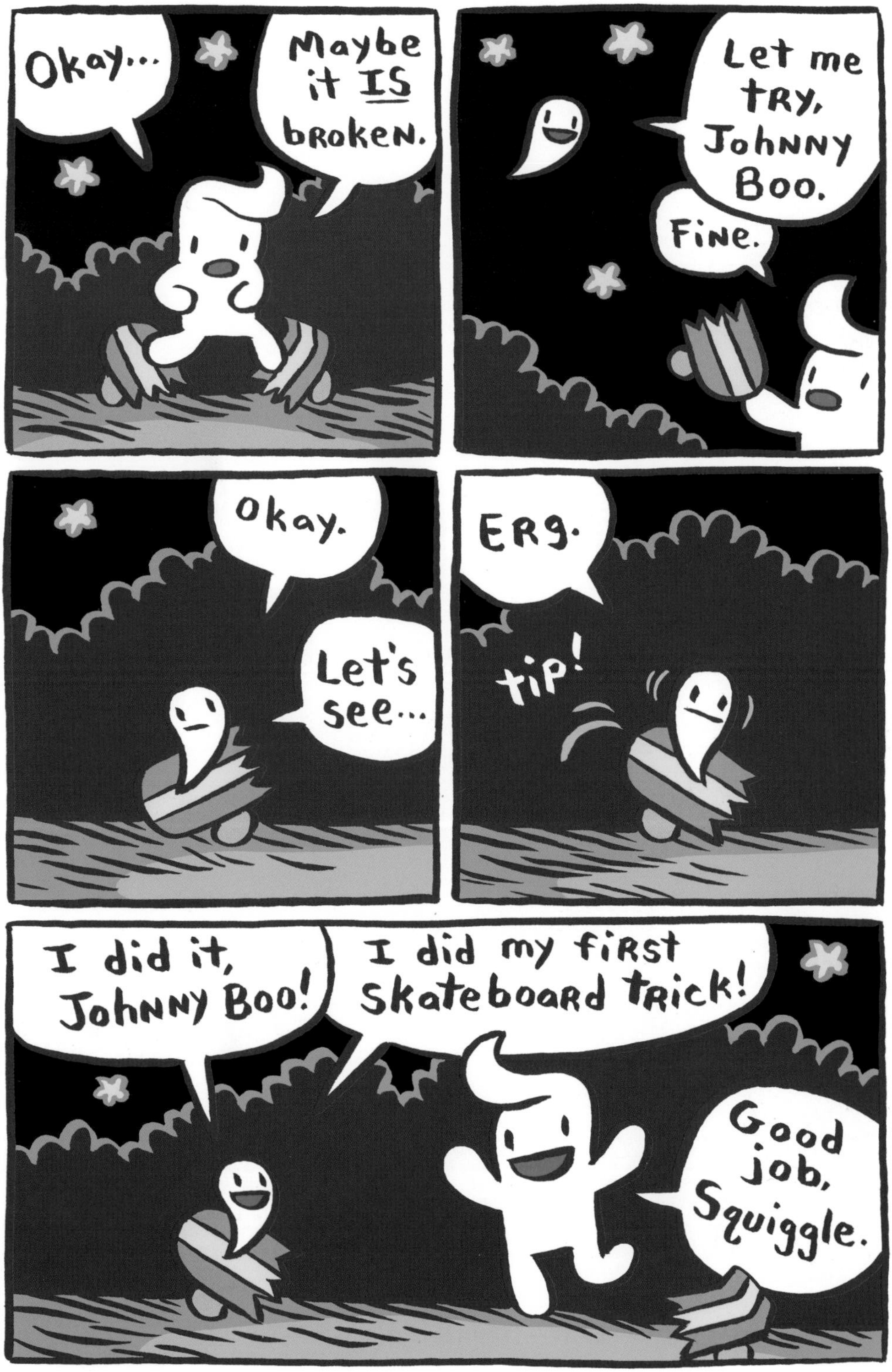
Okay...
Maybe it IS broken.
Let me try, Johnny Boo.
Fine.
Okay.
Let's see...
Erg.
tip!
I did it, Johnny Boo!
I did my first skateboard trick!
Good job, Squiggle.

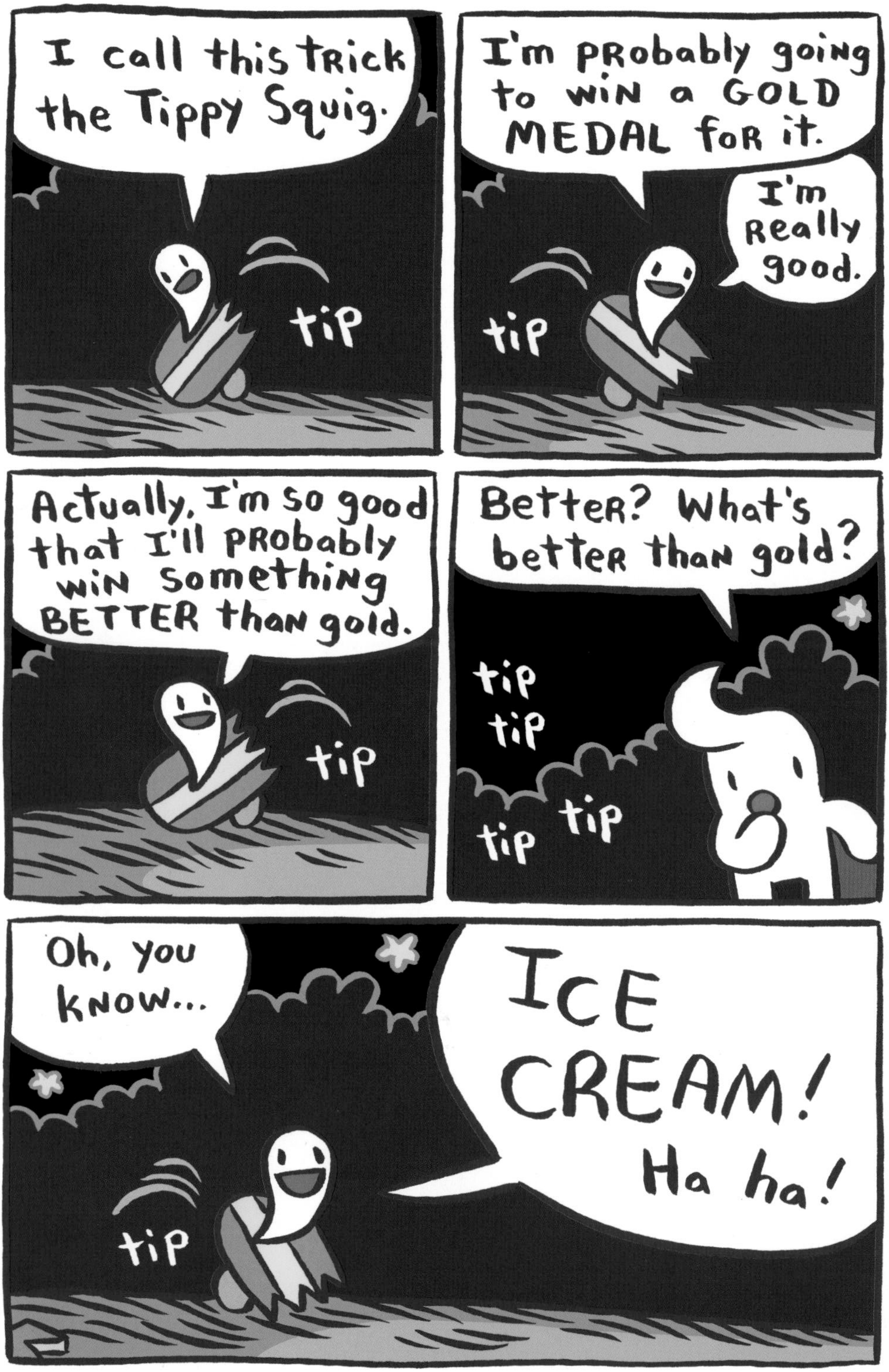
I call this trick the Tippy Squig.
tip
I'm probably going to win a GOLD MEDAL for it.
I'm really good.
tip
Actually, I'm so good that I'll probably win something BETTER than gold.
tip
Better? What's better than gold?
tip
tip
tip
tip
Oh, you know...
ICE CREAM! Ha ha!
tip

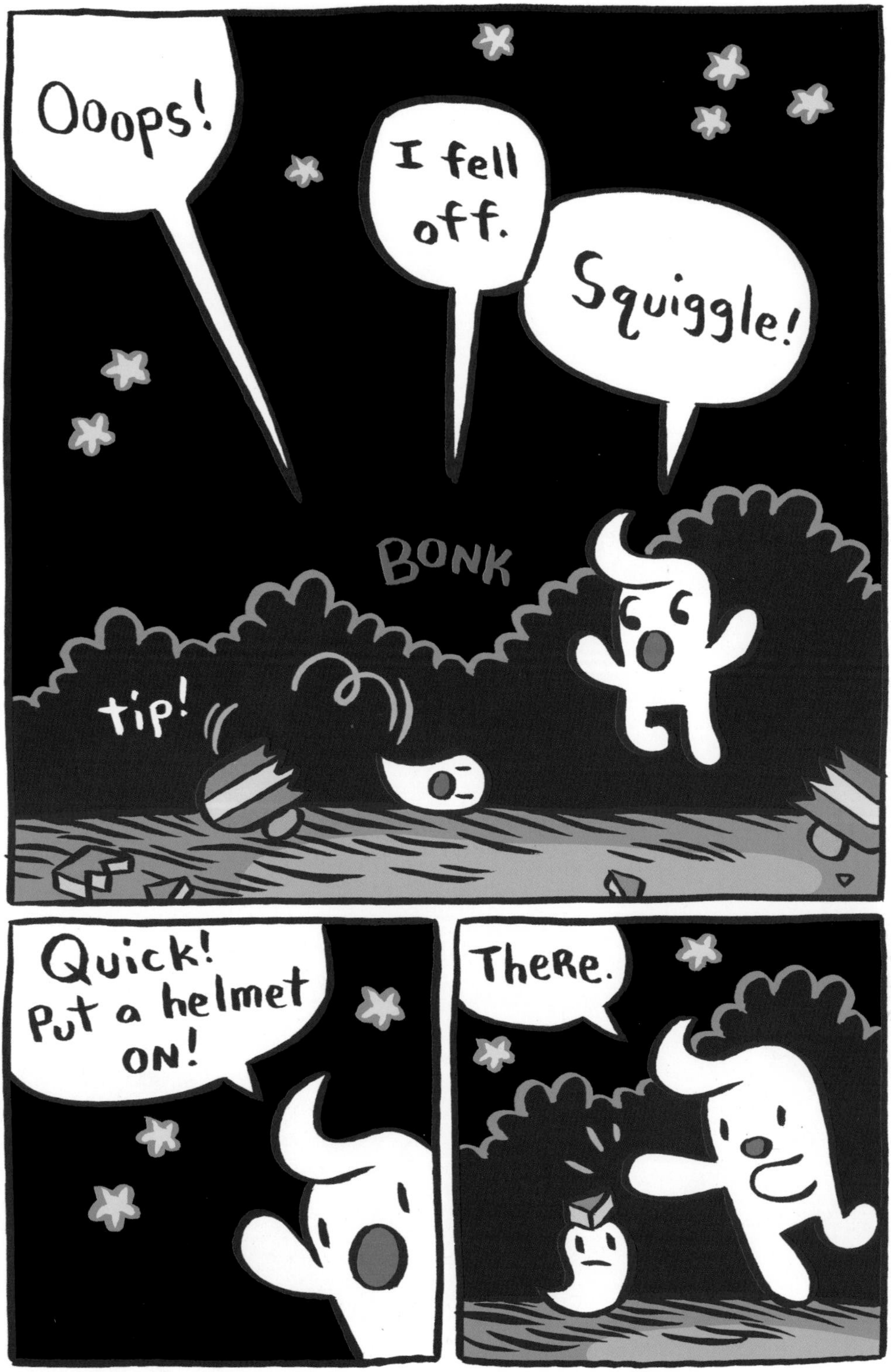
Ooops!
I fell off.
Squiggle!
BONK
tip!
Quick! Put a helmet ON!
There.

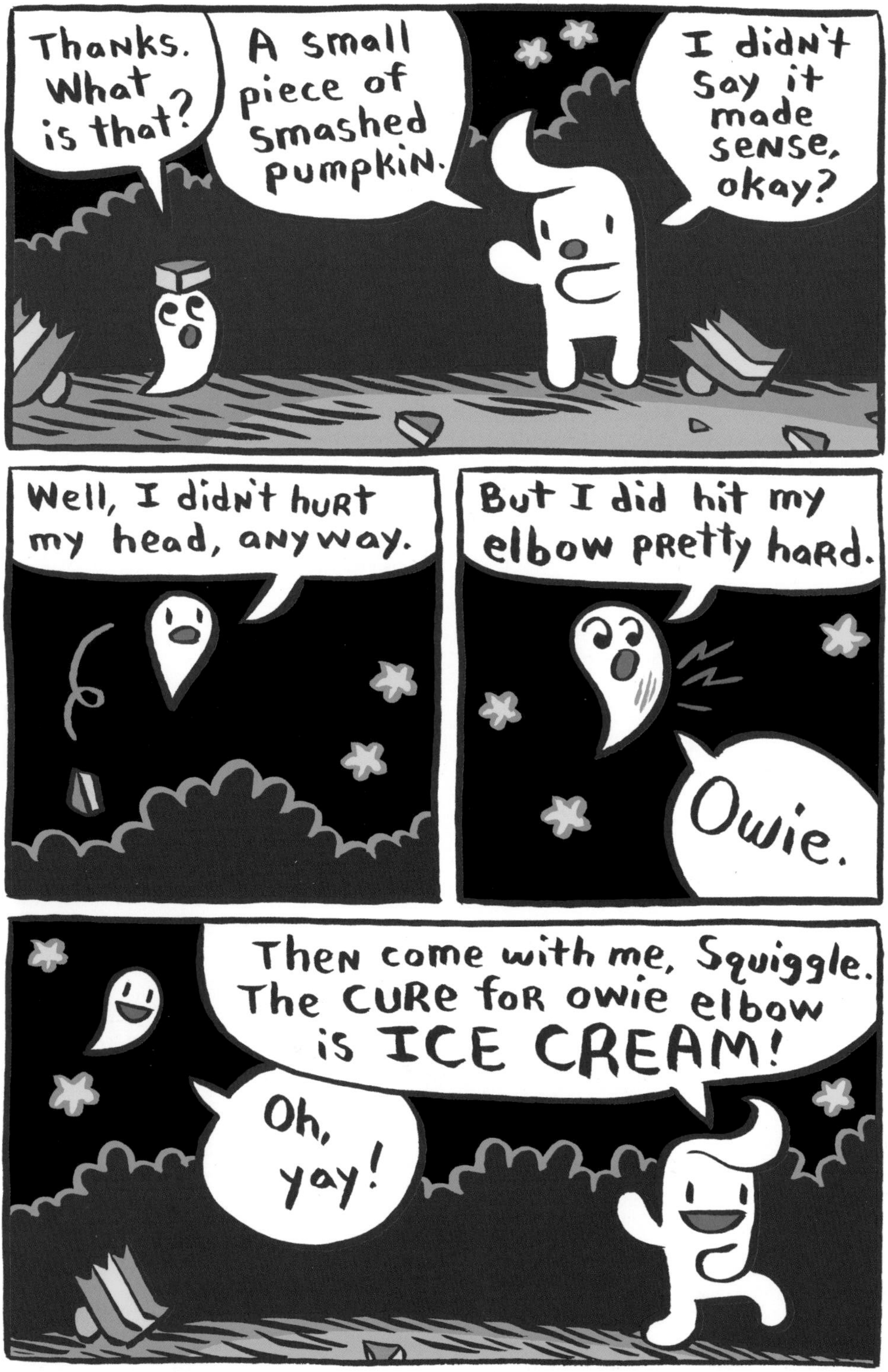
Thanks. What is that?
A small piece of smashed pumpkin.
I didn't say it made sense, okay?
Well, I didn't hurt my head, anyway.
But I did hit my elbow pretty hard.
Owie.
Then come with me, Squiggle. The cure for owie elbow is ICE CREAM!
Oh, yay!

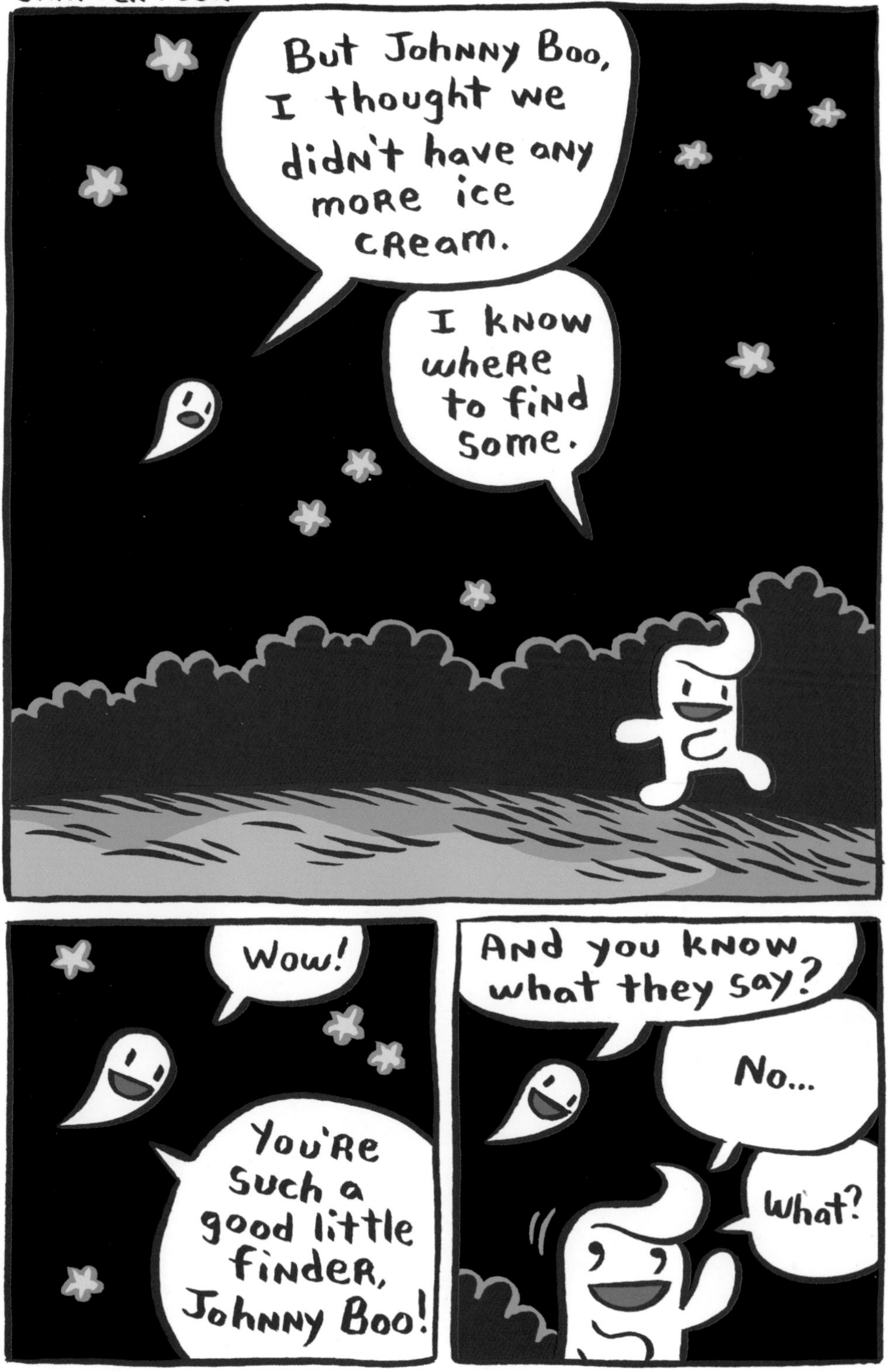
But Johnny Boo, I thought we didn't have any more ice cream.
I know where to find some.
Wow!
You're such a good little finder, Johnny Boo!
And you know what they say?
No...
What?

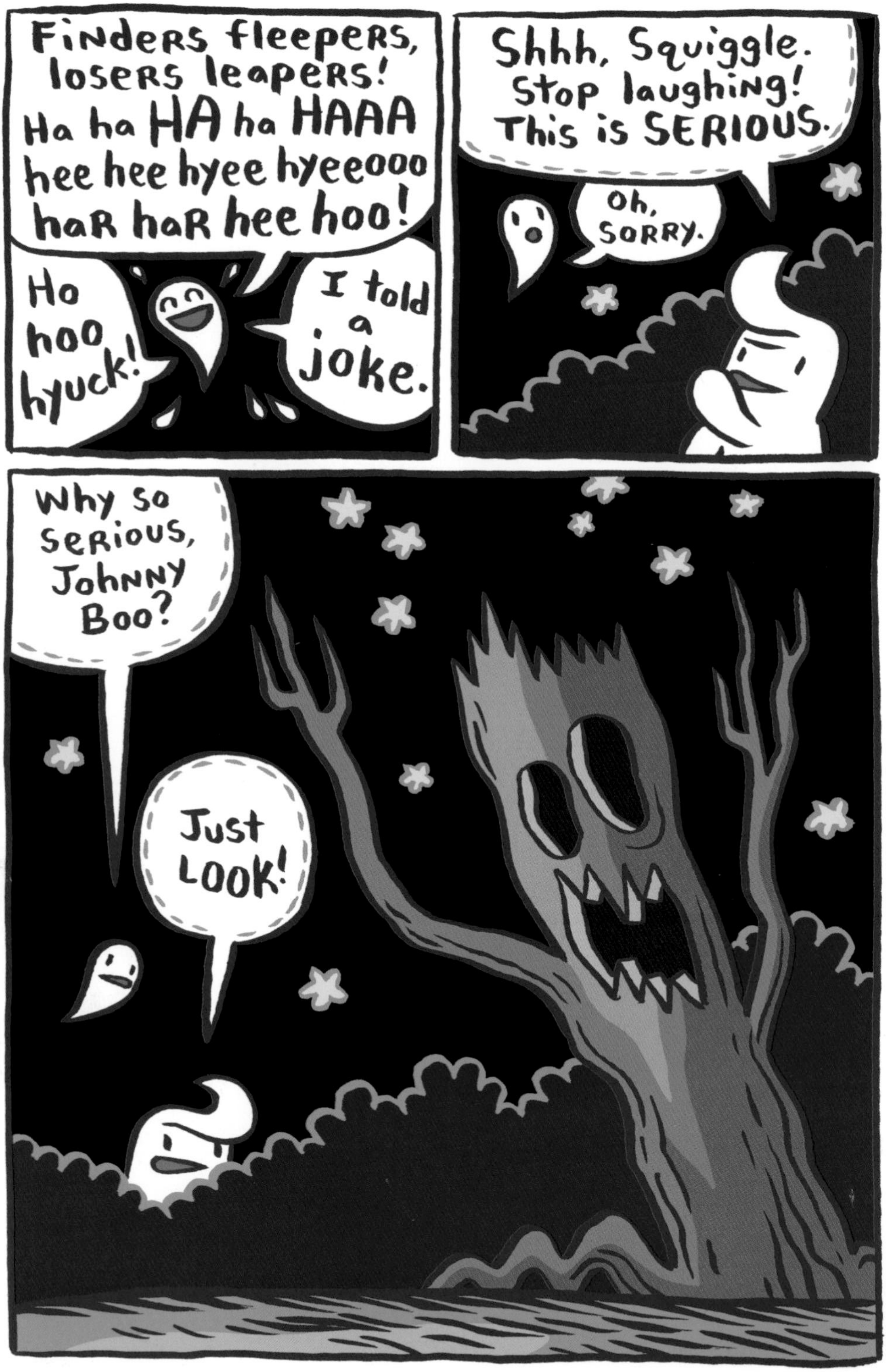
Finders fleepers, losers leapers! Ha ha HA ha HAAA hee hee hyee hyeeooo har har hee hoo!
Ho hoo hyuck!
I told a joke.
Shhh, Squiggle. Stop laughing! This is SERIOUS.
Oh, SORRY.
Why so serious, Johnny Boo?
Just LOOK!

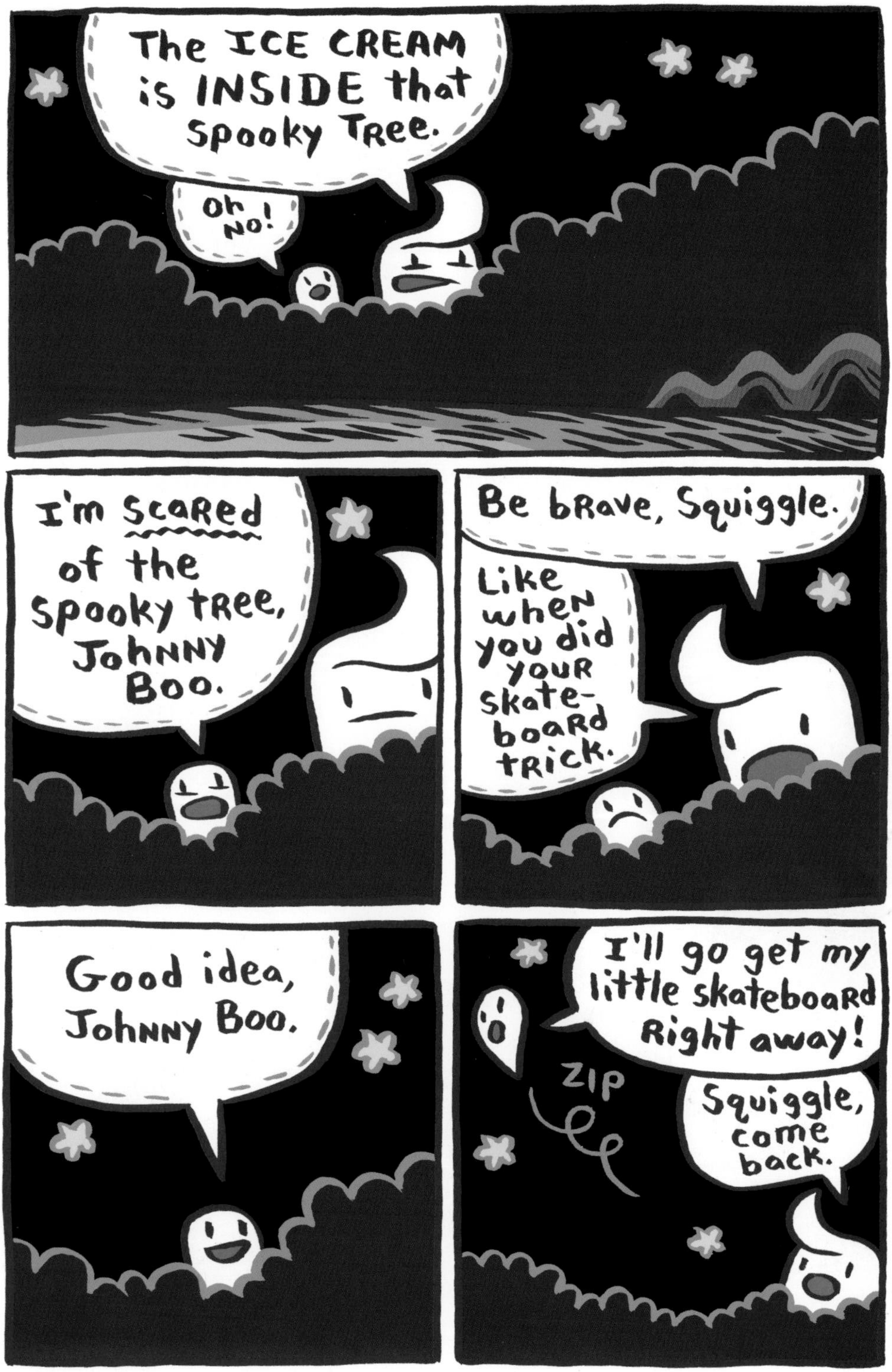
The ICE CREAM is INSIDE that spooky TRee.
Oh NO!
I'm scared of the spooky tRee, JohNNy Boo.
Be bRave, Squiggle.
Like when you did your skate-board tRick.
Good idea, JohNNy Boo.
I'll go get my little skateboaRd Right away!
ZIP
Squiggle, come back.

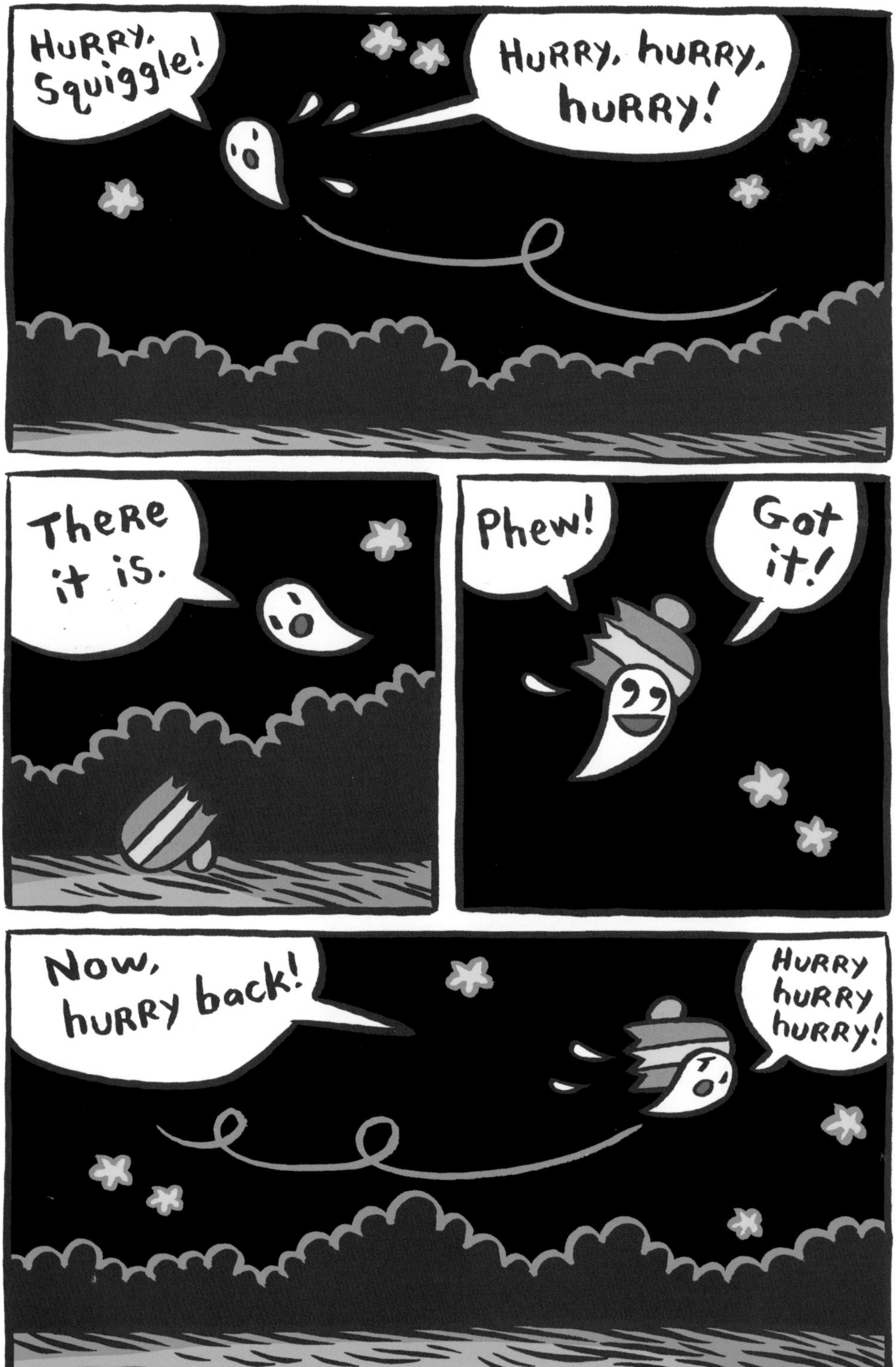
Hurry, Squiggle!
Hurry, hurry, hurry!
There it is.
Phew!
Got it!
Now, hurry back!
Hurry hurry hurry!

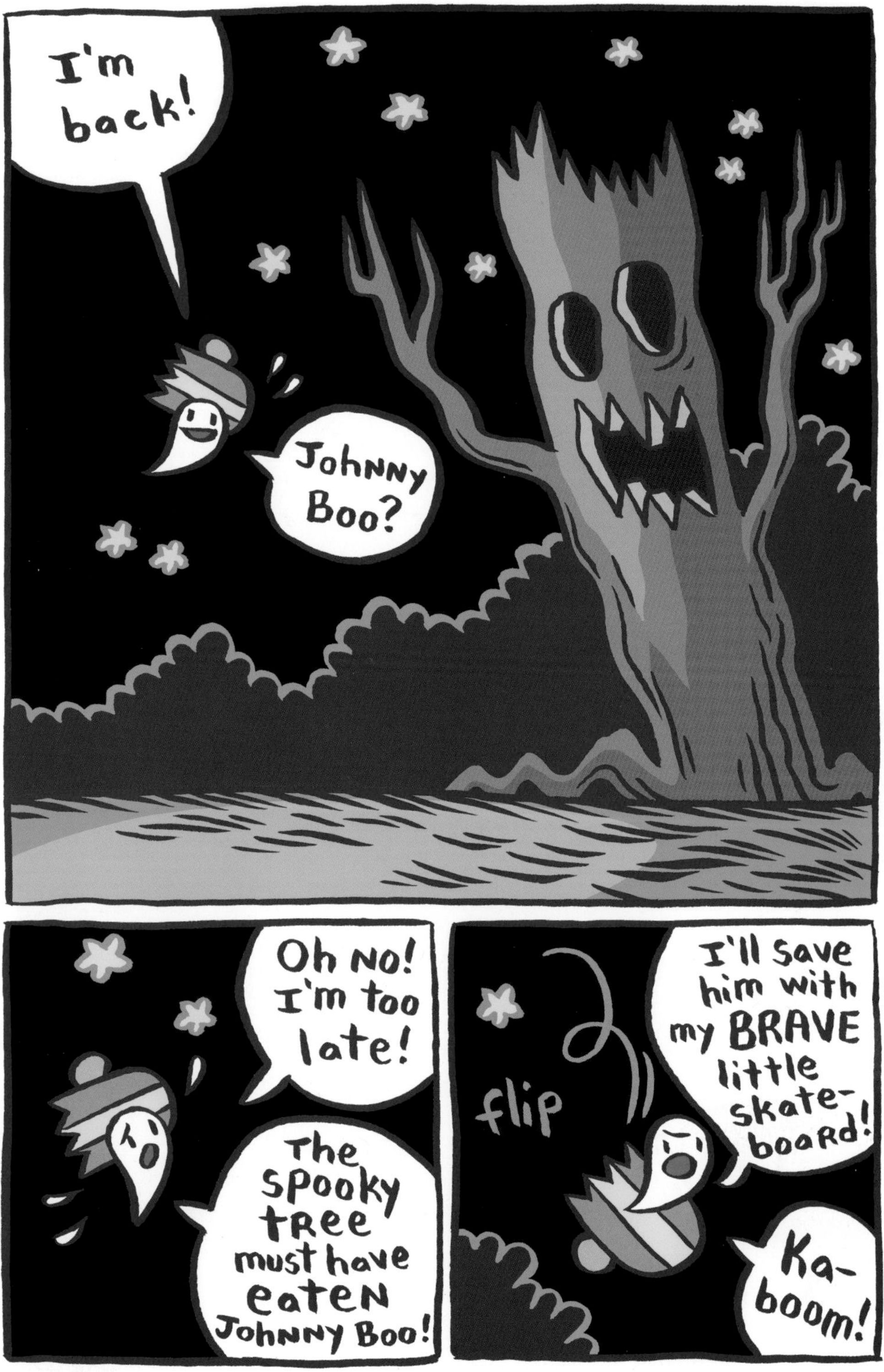
I'm back!
Johnny Boo?
Oh no! I'm too late!
The spooky tree must have eaten Johnny Boo!
flip
I'll save him with my BRAVE little skate-board!
Ka-boom!

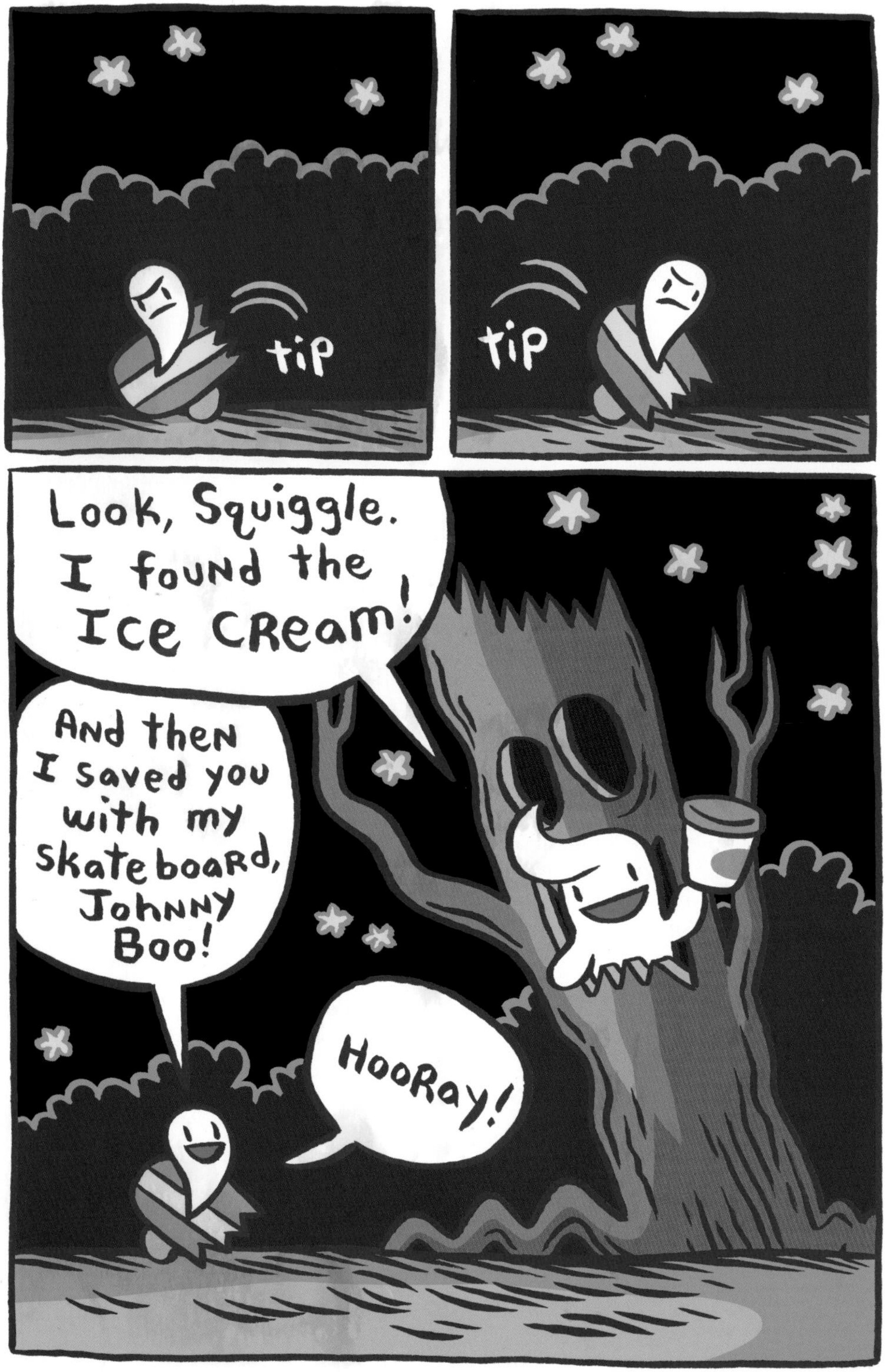
tip
tip
Look, Squiggle. I found the Ice Cream!
And then I saved you with my skateboard, Johnny Boo!
HooRay!

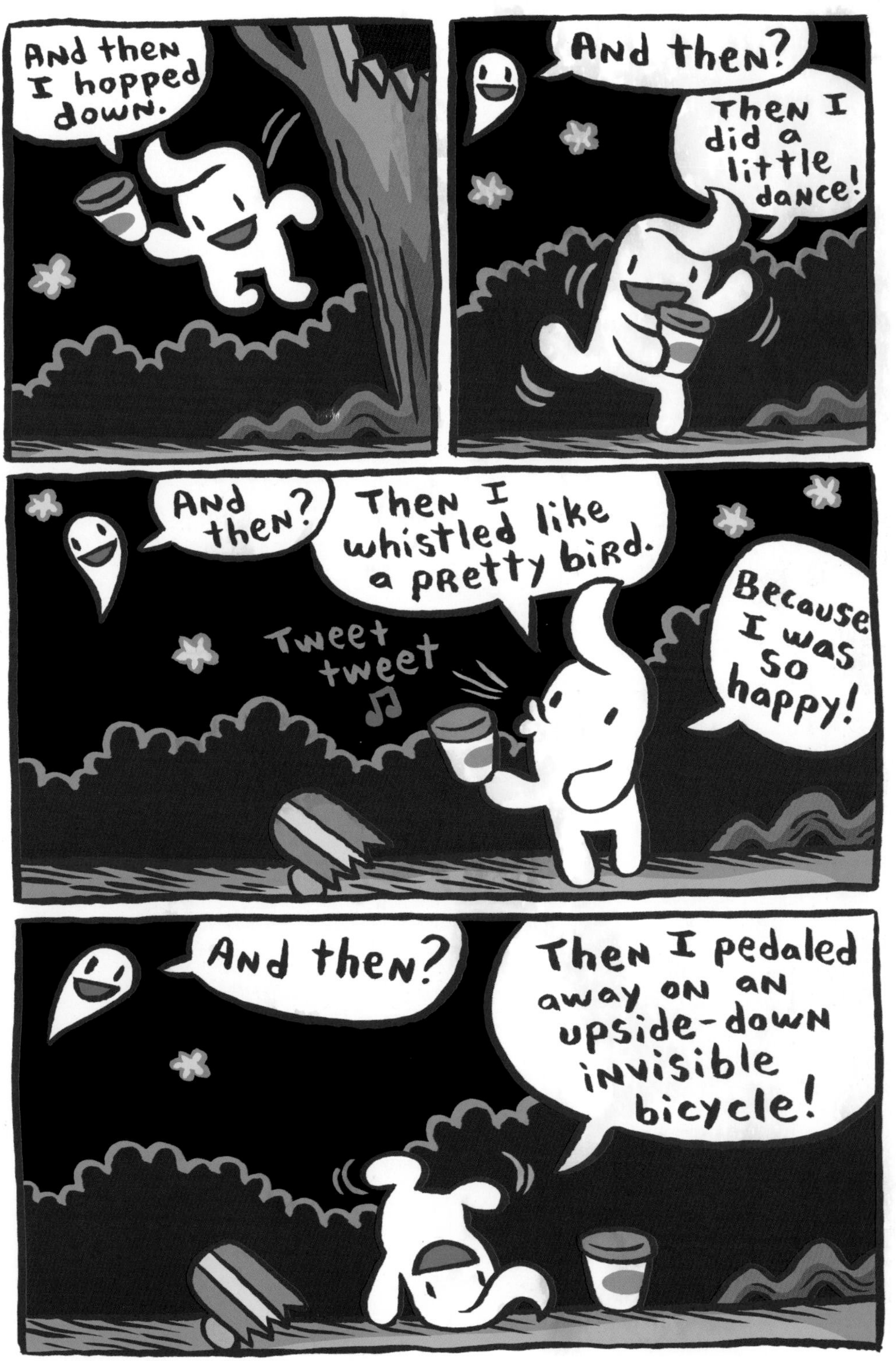
And then I hopped down.
And then?
Then I did a little dance!
And then?
Then I whistled like a pretty bird.
Tweet tweet
Because I was so happy!
And then?
Then I pedaled away on an upside-down invisible bicycle!

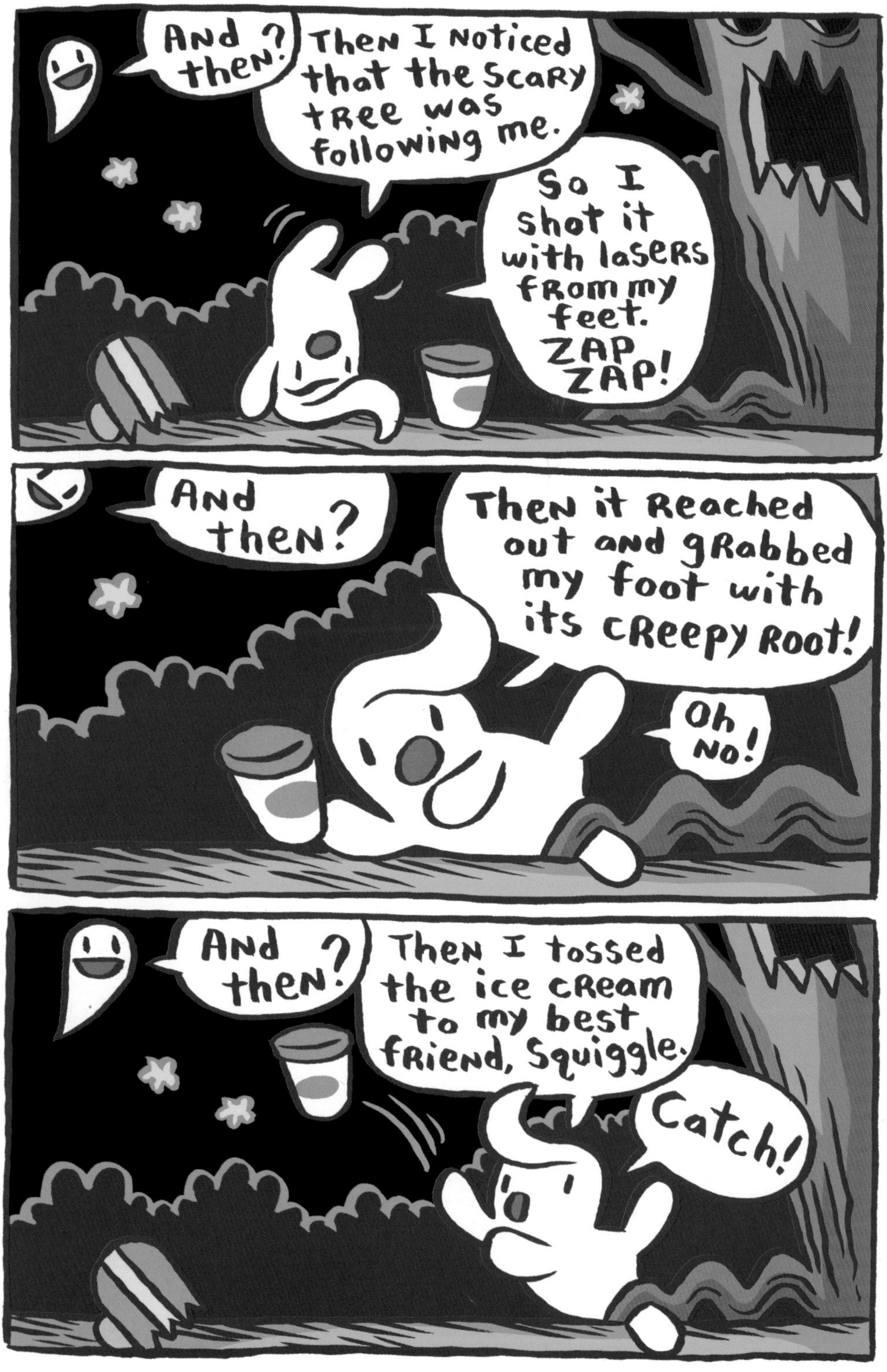
And then?
Then I noticed that the scary tree was following me.
So I shot it with lasers from my feet. ZAP ZAP!
And then?
Then it reached out and grabbed my foot with its creepy root!
Oh no!
And then?
Then I tossed the ice cream to my best friend, Squiggle.
Catch!

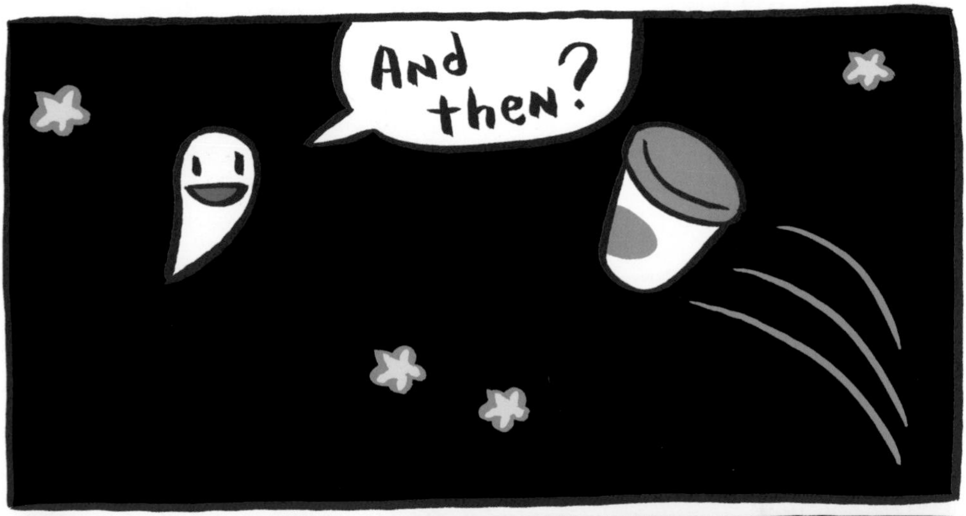
And then?

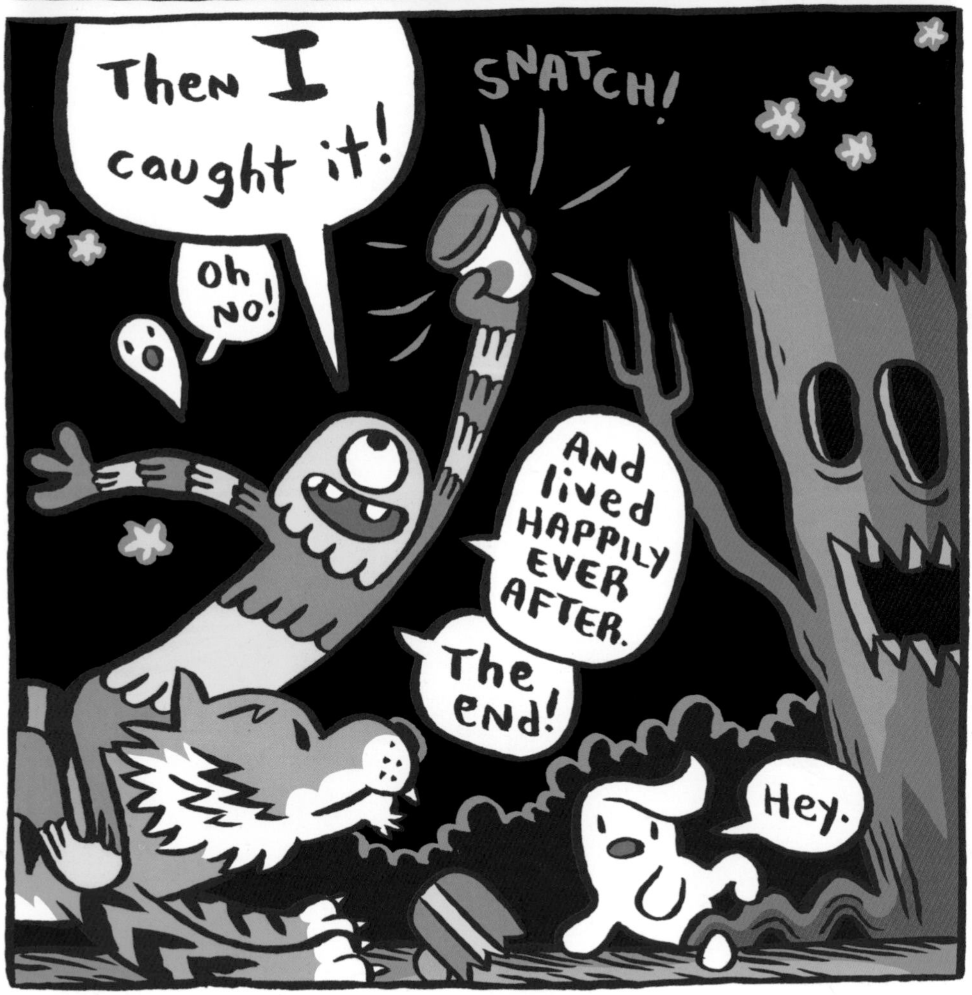
Then I caught it!
SNATCH!
Oh no!
And lived HAPPILY EVER AFTER.
The end!
Hey.

CHAPTER FIVE

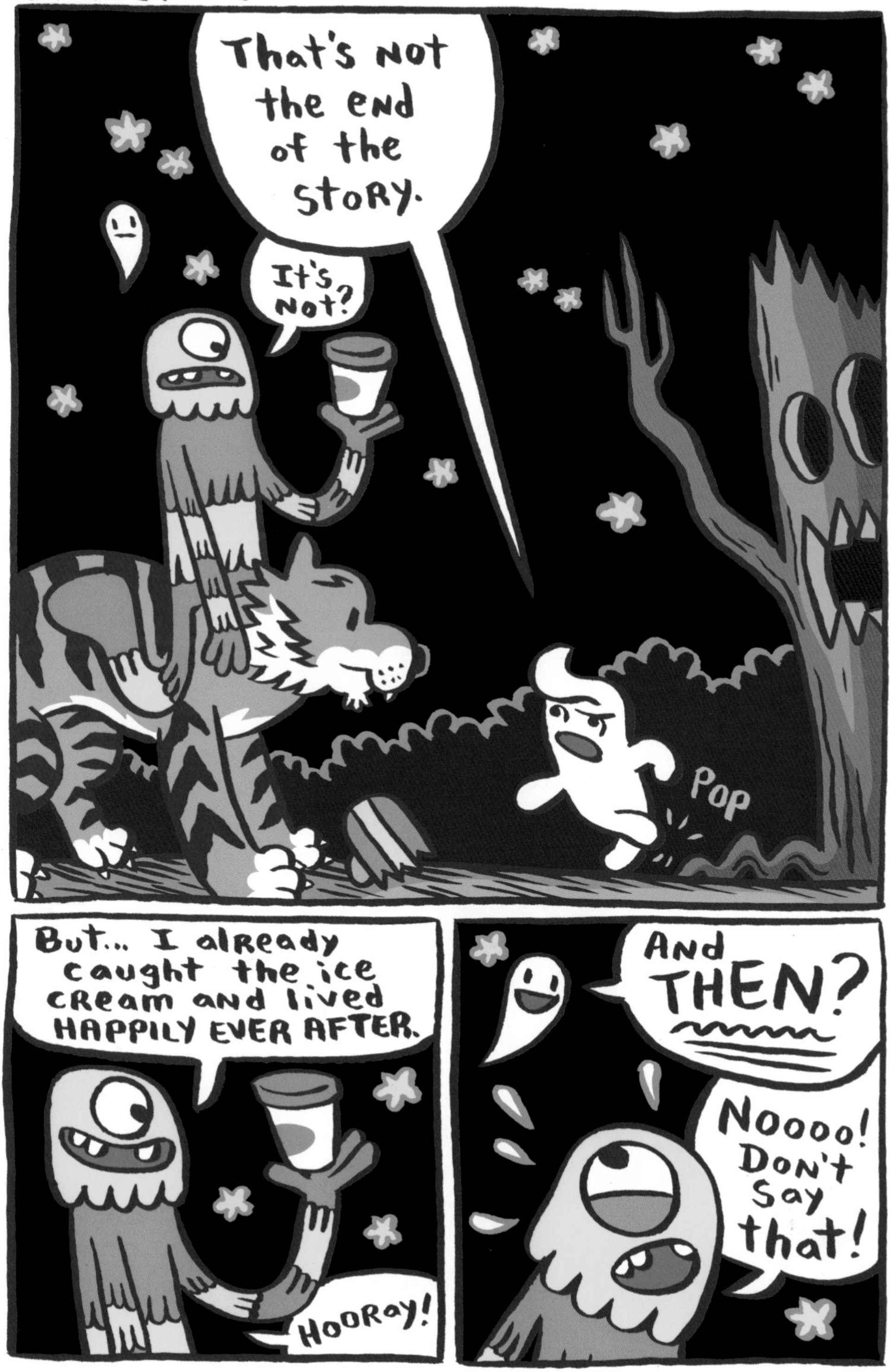
That's not the end of the story.
It's not?
Pop
But... I already caught the ice cream and lived HAPPILY EVER AFTER.
HOORAY!
And THEN?
Noooo! Don't say that!

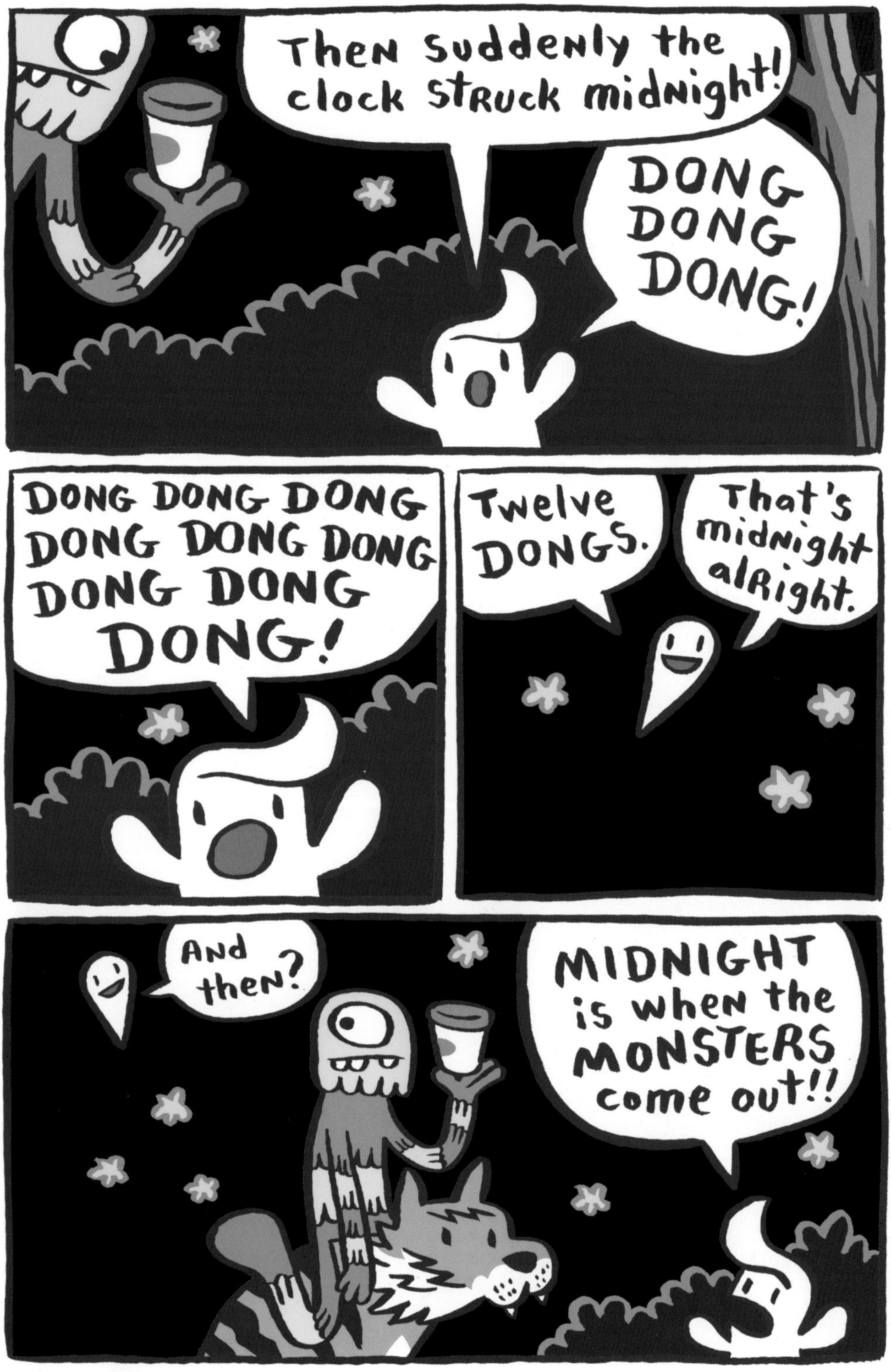
Then suddenly the clock struck midnight!
DONG DONG DONG!
DONG DONG DONG DONG DONG DONG DONG DONG DONG!
Twelve DONGS.
That's midnight alright.
And then?
MIDNIGHT is when the MONSTERS come out!!

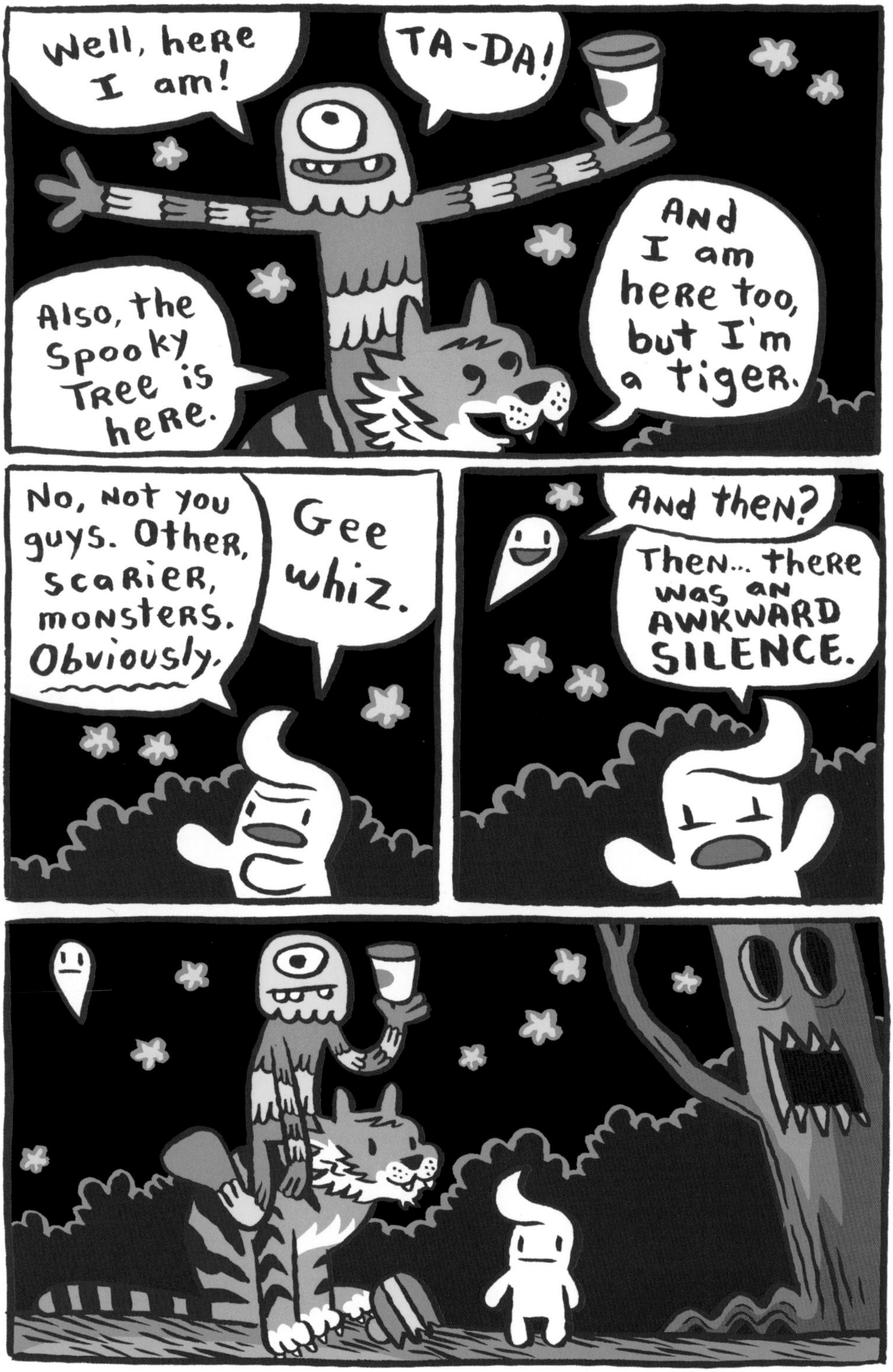
Well, here I am!
TA-DA!
Also, the Spooky Tree is here.
And I am here too, but I'm a tiger.
No, not you guys. Other, scarier, monsters. Obviously.
Gee whiz.
And then?
Then... there was an AWKWARD SILENCE.

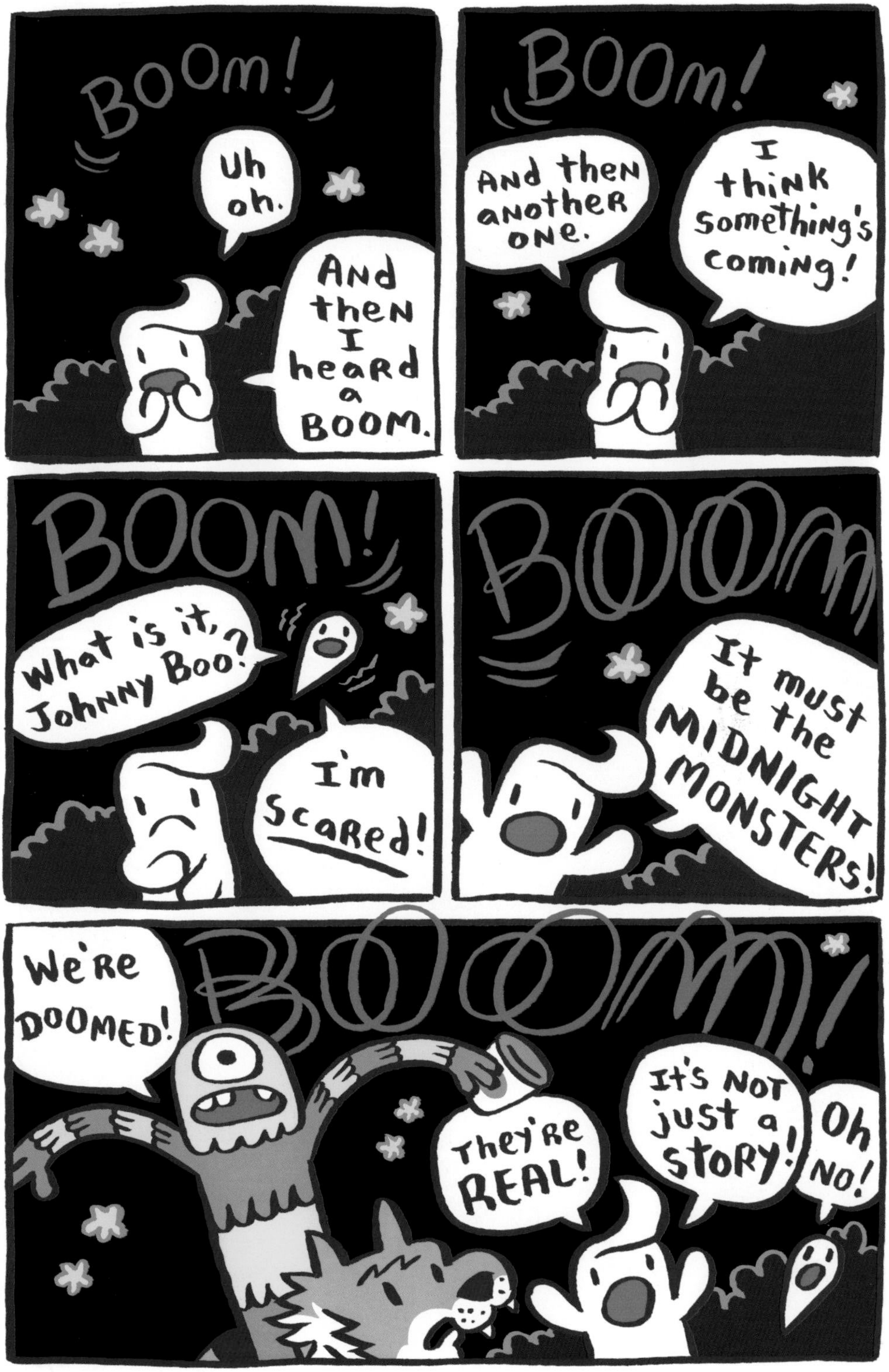
BOOM!
Uh oh.
And then I heard a BOOM.
BOOM!
And then another one.
I think something's coming!
BOOM!
What is it, Johnny Boo?
I'm scared!
BOOOM
It must be the MIDNIGHT MONSTERS!
We're DOOMED!
BOOOM!
They're REAL!
It's NOT just a STORY!
Oh NO!

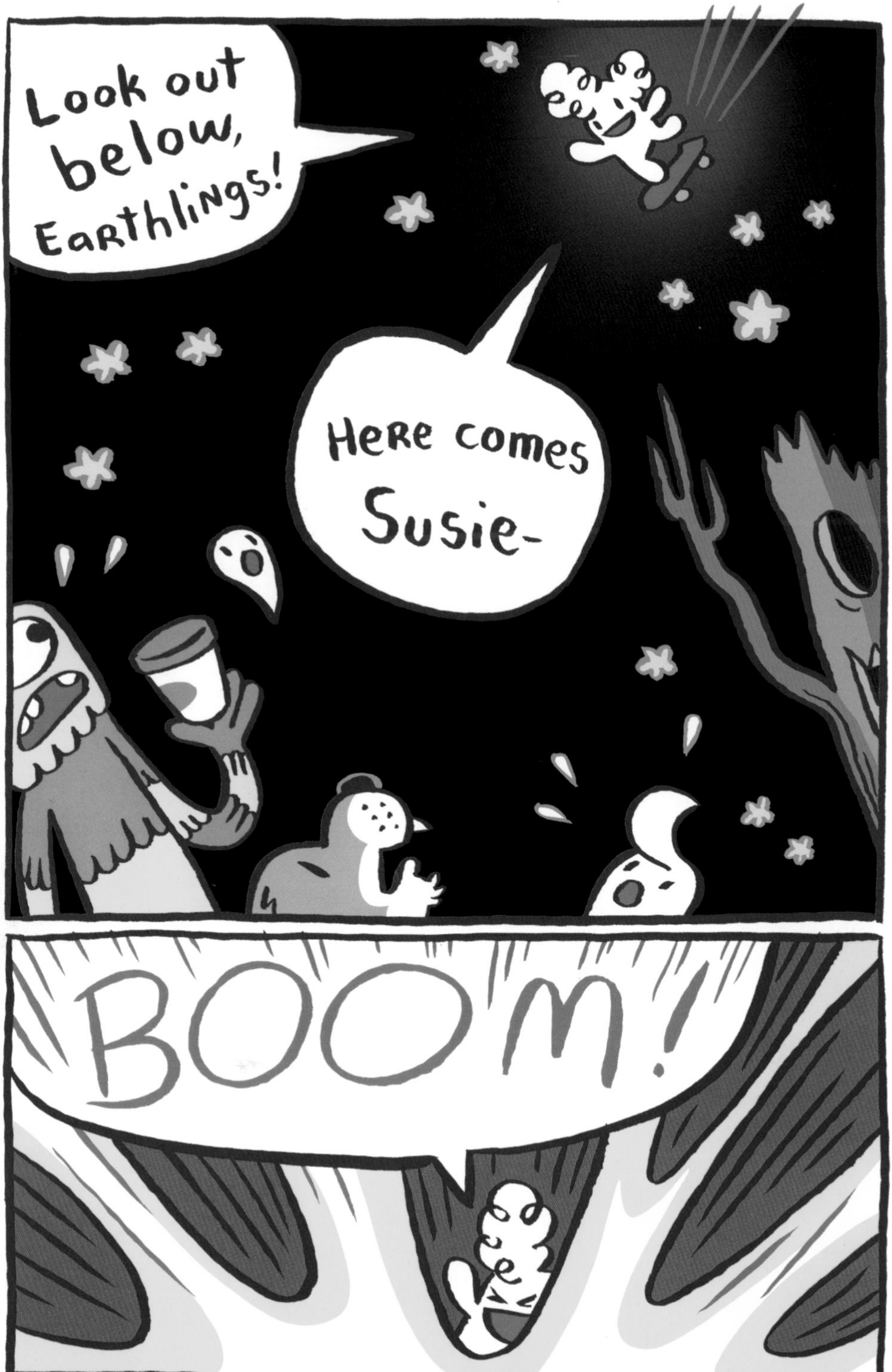
Look out below, Earthlings!
Here comes Susie-
BOOM!

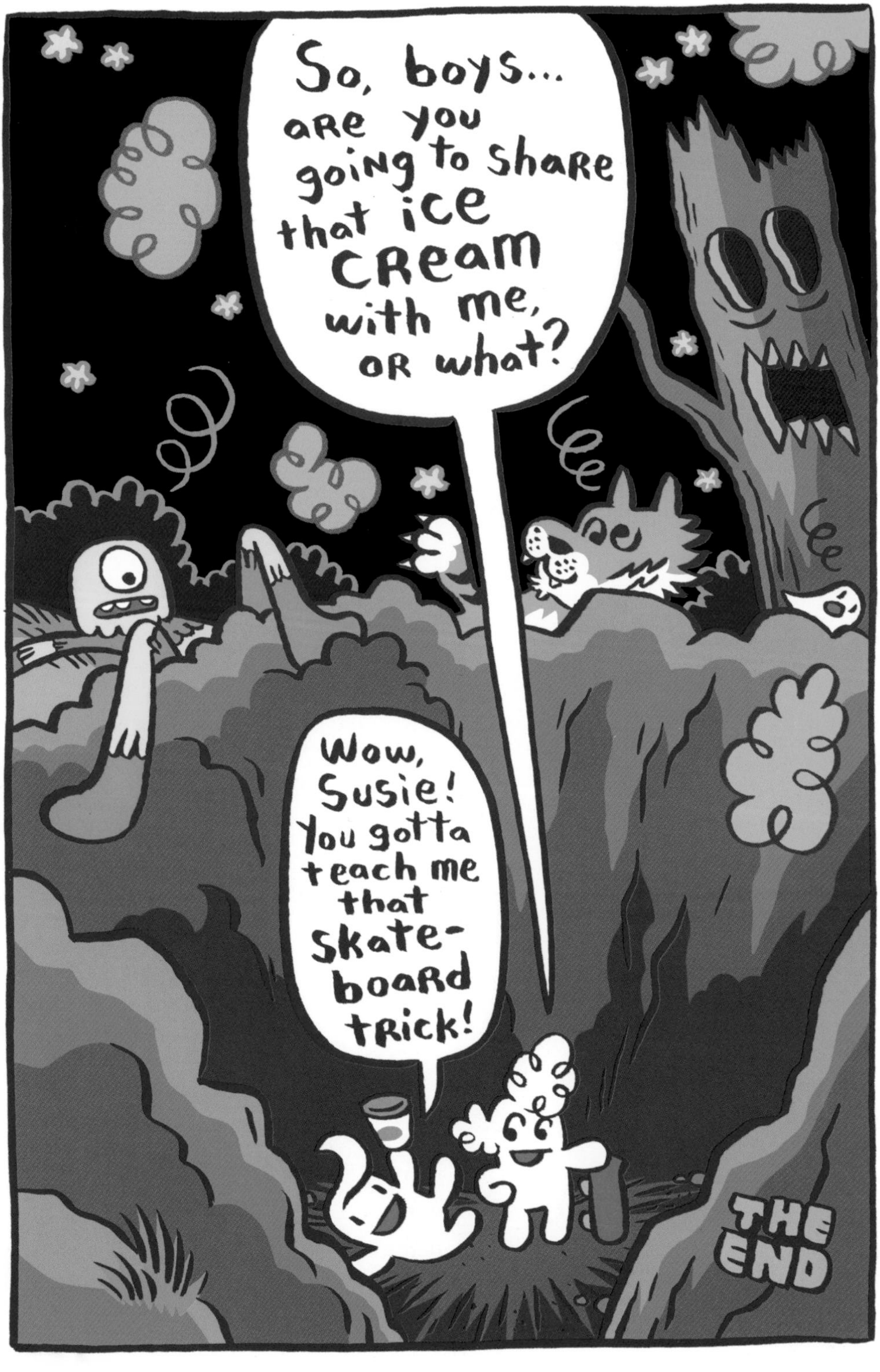
So, boys... are you going to share that ice CREAM with me, OR what?
Wow, Susie! You gotta teach me that Skate-board trick!
THE END

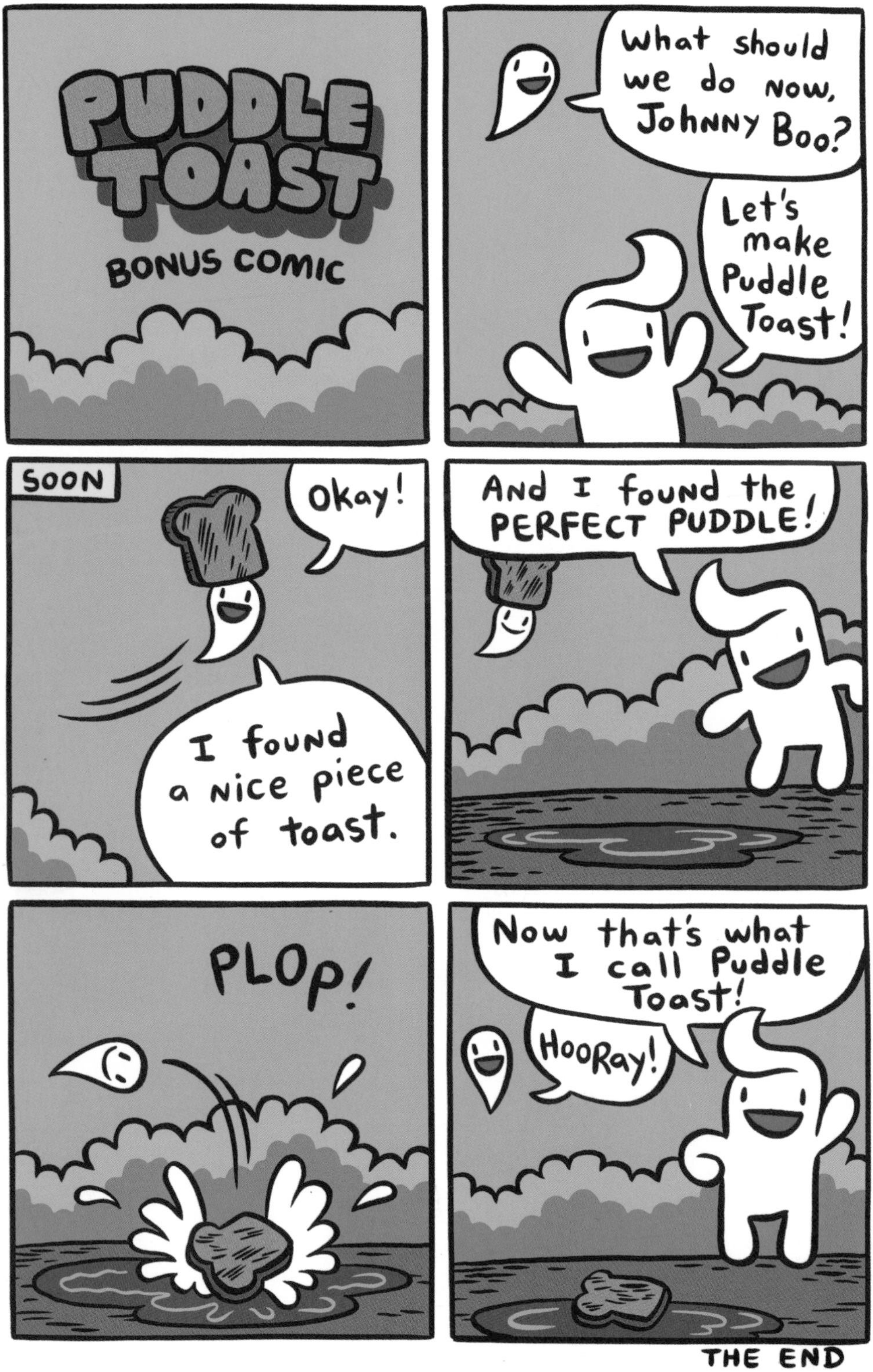
PUDDLE TOAST
BONUS COMIC
What should we do now, Johnny Boo?
Let's make Puddle Toast!
SOON
Okay!
I found a nice piece of toast.
And I found the PERFECT PUDDLE!
PLOP!
Now that's what I call Puddle Toast!
HOORAY!
THE END